A Beautiful Sight

Sandi Lynn

A Beautiful Sight

Photo & Cover Design by: Sara Eirew @ Sara Eirew Photography

Models: Tanner Chidester & Tiffany Marie

Editing by B.Z. Hercules

Books by Sandi Lynn

If you haven't already done so, please check out my other books. They are filled with heartwarming love stories, some with millionaires, and some with just regular everyday people who find love when they least expect it.

Millionaires:
The Forever Series (Forever Black, Forever You, Forever Us, Being Julia, Collin, A Forever Christmas, A Forever Family)
Love, Lust & A Millionaire (Wyatt Brothers, Book 1)
Love, Lust & Liam (Wyatt Brothers, Book 2)
His Proposed Deal
Lie Next To Me (A Millionaire's Love, Book 1)
When I Lie with You (A Millionaire's Love, Book 2)
A Love Called Simon
Then You Happened
The Seduction of Alex Parker
Something About Lorelei
One Night In London
The Exception
Corporate A$$

Second Chance Love:
Remembering You
She Writes Love
Love In Between (Love Series, Book 1)
The Upside of Love (Love Series, Book 2)

Sports:
Lightning

Table of Contents

Chapter 1
Ethan

"What the fuck do you mean you can't make it work?" I shouted as I walked around the long rectangular table.

"I'm sorry, Ethan, but we've tried everything," Jarod spoke.

"Obviously you didn't because I know damn well we can do this. Do you think I pay you well to sit there and tell me that it can't be done? We are on the verge of a breakthrough here. A breakthrough that will make this company billions of dollars."

"But, Ethan—"

"No buts!" I shouted as I pointed at Jarod. "Google hasn't released their product yet. It's still in beta testing and you know every other damn technology company out there is working on the same thing. I want ours to be the first and the best. It's not rocket science. It's technology. Every one of you," I pointed to the group of men and women sitting around the table, "is an MIT graduate. This is what you do. It's shit like this that keeps you up at night."

"Ethan, we've tried several times," Edward spoke.

"Try again and keep trying until you figure it out." I scowled. "You have thirty more days." I shook my head as I walked out and slammed the door.

Fuck. I didn't need this shit today. Walking back to my office, I yelled for Holly, my assistant.

"Yes, Mr. Klein?" she nervously spoke.

Taking a seat behind my desk, I picked up the time-off request form she filled out.

"What's this?" I asked as I held up the piece of paper.

"It's my and my husband's one-year wedding anniversary and we wanted to take a trip to Hawaii."

"Didn't you go to Hawaii for your honeymoon?" I glared at her.

"Yes. We wanted to go back."

"Well, the dates you are requesting don't work for me. I have a lot going on during that time and I'll need you here. Go to dinner and have a night of wild sex. That's all you need to celebrate."

"But, sir, it's our one year."

"Congratulations. You made it a whole year. Big deal. When it's your twenty-fifth, let me know and maybe I'll give you the time off to celebrate. But until then, the answer is no. I need you here."

She lowered her head because she didn't want me to see the tears that formed in her eyes.

"Get out of here and get back to work."

She turned and walked out of my office, carefully closing the door behind her. Shaking my head, I picked up my phone from my desk and noticed a text message from Samantha.

"Hey there, sexy. Want to come over tonight?"

"I can't tonight. I promised Charles that I would go to some art gallery thing. How fast can you get to the Plaza Hotel? I have a lot of tension I need to release right now."

"I can be there in fifteen minutes."

"Good. You know which room. I'm leaving now. It would be wise if you didn't wear any panties. I already owe you five pairs as it is."

"I won't wear any. I'll see you soon."

Walking out of my office, I stopped at Lucy's, my secretary's, desk.

"I'm leaving the office. I'll be back in about an hour and a half."

"Yes, sir. By the way, Holly looks pretty upset."

"She'll get over it." I walked away.

Climbing into the limo, I shut the door, and Harry, my driver, glanced at me through the rearview mirror.

"The Plaza Hotel," I spoke as I pulled out my phone.

"Who are you meeting this time?"

"Samantha."

"I don't care for her," he spoke.

"And I don't pay you to care for the women I see. Do I?"

"No you don't. But I'm giving you my opinion anyway." He smirked.

"Keep your opinions to yourself."

"Shit, Ethan. *You* don't even like half the girls you fuck."

"I don't have to like them, Harry. I just like what's between their legs."

He sighed and slowly shook his head. As we pulled up to the curb of the Plaza Hotel, the doorman opened the door for me and I climbed out.

"Good afternoon, Mr. Klein."

"Hello, Don."

"Enjoy your stay."

"I intend to." I smirked.

I headed up to my room on the 19th floor, scanned the keycard, and stepped inside. After taking off my suitcoat, I began to unbutton my shirt when I heard a knock at the door.

"You're late." I glared at Samantha.

"Traffic, Ethan. It's New York. I don't live right around the corner."

She wore a short red dress with high red heels. I could tell she wasn't wearing a bra because her hard nipples poked through the fabric of her dress. I slid my shirt off my shoulders and unbuckled my belt as I walked towards her. Placing my hand between her thighs, I slowly slid it upwards until I reached her pussy and plunged a finger inside. She gasped. I reached around with my other hand and unzipped her dress, letting it fall to the ground.

"Keep your shoes on."

She placed her hand around the nape of my neck and moved her lips closer to mine. I pulled away.

"You know the rules, Samantha. No kissing. Get on all fours on the bed."

She did as I asked while I removed the condom from my wallet. Taking down my pants, I rolled the condom over my hard cock, grabbed hold of her hips, and thrust into her fast and hard. Loud moans escaped her lips. I thrust in and out of her rapidly, while the wetness that emerged from her enveloped my cock. Unpinning her hair, I grabbed onto it.

"Do you like when I do this?" I pulled her hair.

"Yes. Oh yes."

After pulling her hair a few more times, I let go and reached around to her breasts, pinching her nipples, which caused her moans to grow even louder.

"What do I like to hear?" I asked as I pounded into her.

"Harder, Ethan. Fuck me harder."

After a few more thrusts, I pulled out of her and turned her on her back, pushing her legs up as far as they would go, allowing my cock to go deeper inside her. The buildup was coming and I welcomed it. I needed it. After a few more hard, deep thrusts, I halted and moaned as I came and all the tension that I felt was released.

Climbing off of her, I went into the bathroom and disposed of the condom.

"Are you okay?" I asked as I grabbed my shirt off the floor and put it on.

"Yeah. I'm great." She smiled. "Why won't you let me kiss you?" she asked as she lay on the bed.

"Because I don't need to be kissed, Samantha. You know the rules. Don't ask again." I slipped on my pants.

"Do you have to leave already?" she pouted.

"You know how busy I am. I have to get back to the office."

"You're always busy, Ethan. Have you ever thought about slowing down and smelling the roses every once in a while?"

"Nah." I smiled. "As long as there's money to be made, there's work to be done."

"I hate you," she spoke.

"No you don't. If you did, you wouldn't keep coming back for more." I adjusted my tie as I looked in the mirror.

"The sex is great. That's why I keep coming back for more. But as for you, you're an emotionless bastard."

"I know and that's the way I like it. Enjoy the rest of your day, Samantha." I winked as I walked out the door.

My life was all about my company and about control. My employees and colleagues referred to me as the "Iceman" because I had nothing but ice running through my veins. Emotions weren't my thing, feelings were non-existent, and my own gain was top priority, no matter who I had to step on to get what I wanted. It was how I became so successful, building and running a billion-dollar technology company by the age of thirty. I was on top and that was all that mattered to me.

Chapter 2
Aubrey

After running a brush through my long blonde hair, I slipped into my brand new strapless, black and white floral print, A-line waist dress. Tonight was a special night because my best friend, Penelope, was having her very first exhibition at a well-known art gallery.

Penelope Carson and I had met in college when I accidentally bumped into her and knocked all of her books out of her hands. Sometimes, I could be really clumsy. She forgave me, we had coffee, and a friendship was formed.

As I was getting my shoes from the closet, I heard the front door open and my Aunt Charlotte's voice filtered through the apartment.

"I was at the store and picked you up some fruit and some more K-cups," she yelled.

"Thank you." I smiled as I walked towards the kitchen.

"Ah. Penelope's art exhibition is tonight, isn't it?" She grabbed hold of my hands.

"Yes. Ian should be here soon."

"You look beautiful, Aubrey. That dress is perfect."

"Thanks. Penelope helped me pick it out."

The front door opened and my other best friend, Ian, walked in.

"Wow. Who's that sexy woman standing right before me?"

"Oh stop, Ian. You know I'm way too old for you," Aunt Charlotte spoke.

"Damn, Charlotte. You're always turning me down."

"You two have fun and tell Penelope that I said congratulations."

"We will." I gave her a kiss on the cheek.

"Are you ready to go, Madame?" Ian asked.

"I'm very ready." I hooked my arm in his and we walked out the door.

****

Ethan

The last place I wanted to go tonight was an art exhibition. But I promised my friend, Charles, that I would go with him since his girlfriend, Lexi, was out of town visiting her parents. He was an art fanatic and always looking for something new.

"Will you relax, Ethan?" Charles spoke as he placed his hand on my shoulder.

"I'm fine, Charles. I just had a bad day at the office. Everything that could go wrong did, and I lost a lot of money."

"What did you lose? A million or two? That's chump change, my friend." He smirked.

"Money is money." I sighed.

"By the way, Lexi wanted me to tell you that when she gets back, she's introducing you to her friend, Greta. She wants us to double date."

"Tell her no thanks. I'm not interested."

"She's smoking hot, man. Tall, toned, long dark brown hair, exotic eyes. She looks like she just stepped out of a *Playboy* magazine. I'd totally fuck her if I wasn't with Lexi."

"I have plenty of women I fuck. I don't need to get involved with a friend of Lexi's. That's just asking for trouble."

"Doesn't matter. Lexi already thinks you're a douchebag." He smiled. "Ethan, it's been—"

"Don't, Charles. You know exactly where I stand. Now change the subject or I'm leaving." I scowled.

"Fine. It's your life. Be miserable."

"I'm not miserable. I live my life the way I want and nobody is going to change that."

He rolled his eyes at me and sighed. "Let's go look at some art."

I grabbed a glass of champagne from the waiter as he passed by holding up a tray and decided to take a look at what this new artist had to offer. Since I was here, I might as well make use of my time. I left Charles standing as he was looking and went over to the other side of the gallery where a few more paintings were displayed. As I was standing there looking at a specific painting, I heard Charles call my name from across the gallery. When I turned around, I accidentally bumped into a woman who was standing rather closely behind me.

"Oh, excuse me." I lightly placed my hand on her arm and found myself unable to take my eyes off of her.

"I'm sorry. I shouldn't have been standing so close," her innocent voice spoke as she looked down.

"Please, don't apologize. I shouldn't have turned around so quickly."

She was stunning; absolutely gorgeous and absolutely fuckable. She stood about five foot eight, had beautiful long blonde hair, emerald eyes, and from what I could see in that dress, the body of a goddess.

"Ethan!" Charles shouted again as he waved his hand in the air.

"Again, I'm sorry." I walked away and headed over to where Charles was.

"What were you doing over there? Who was that woman?" he asked.

"I don't know. I practically knocked her over when I turned around to see what the hell you wanted."

"Oh. Sorry about that. Look at this painting. Isn't it beautiful? Do you think Lexi would like it?"

"Sure. It's nice. Why don't you take a picture of it and send it to her?"

"Nah. I thought about that, but I want it to be a surprise. You know, for when she comes back from Minnesota. A little 'I missed you' gift."

"She's only been gone a week."

"I know. But for us, that's a long time apart." He arched his brow. "I think she'll like it. I'm going to track down the artist and make her night." He smiled.

Charles and I had been best friends since we were ten years old when his family moved into the townhouse next to mine. His parents owned a couple of dry cleaners, which did very well until his father developed a gambling problem and lost everything, including the family home. Charles didn't let it affect him. He was in college at the time getting his financial degree and after he graduated with honors, he went to work as a financial analyst on Wall Street. His girlfriend, Lexi, was a nurse in the ER at Mount Sinai Hospital. They met the night I brought him in after some guy beat the shit out of him for hitting on his girlfriend. In Charles' defense, she left out the fact that she was there with someone. That was over two years ago and he and Lexi have been together ever since. As for me, I loved women, and I used the term lightly. I loved their bodies and the pleasure they gave me. That was about it. I could care less about their feelings, jobs, life, or what they liked to do in their spare time. I was a user, and I used women for what I needed, for what I craved, and for what they could do for me. They were a tension reliever. Some people did meditation, yoga, listened to music, or took pills. Not me. I had sex. Hard, fast, and rough.

I stared across the gallery at the woman I almost knocked over. She was still standing in the same spot staring at that painting.

Chapter 3

Aubrey

I didn't realize I was standing so close to him because I was too focused on his scent, which drew me in. A woodsy smell with a mixture of moss, amber, and a touch of spice. Clean, refreshing, intoxicating. A scent that somehow pulled me from my senses. Standing in the same spot, I held the wine glass in my hand, and as soon as I brought it to my lips, the same scent filtered through the air.

"Hello, again," the familiar low voice from earlier spoke next to me.

"Hello."

"You're still standing in the same spot, staring at that painting. It must really intrigue you."

My lips gave way to a small smile. "A painting can tell a thousand different stories to different people."

"You think so?" he asked.

"Tell me what you see when you look at it," I spoke.

"Well, I see a woman standing at the shore of the dark ocean water underneath a gray sky filled with dark clouds. She's looking up at the small streaks of light that are coming down and glistening over parts of the water."

"What else?" I asked.

"The sand is dark in color except for where there's a lighthouse in the distance, casting its light and lighting a path in the sand."

"And what does this painting say to you?"

"To be honest, I haven't got a clue," he spoke. "What does it say to you?"

"It says that even in a world of darkness, you will always see light."

"That's pretty deep. I can see the artist is very talented and inspirational."

"Yes. She is." I smiled.

****

Ethan

Her voice was soft and angelic. She was beautiful and I wanted to get to know her. But only small details so I could bring her to the Plaza and fuck her senseless.

"I'm Ethan Klein." I extended my hand to her.

"Aubrey Callahan." The corners of her mouth gave way to a shy smile as she placed her hand in mine.

The feel of her soft hand caused my cock to twitch. Enough of a twitch that I had to place my left hand in my pocket to keep it calm.

"There you are," Charles spoke as he walked up to me and placed his hand on my shoulder. "I bought the painting for Lexi. She's going to be so surprised."

"Charles, this is Aubrey Callahan. Aubrey, this is Charles St. John."

"It's nice to meet you, Charles."

"The pleasure is all mine, Aubrey. Have you had a chance to meet the artist, Penelope? She's so nice and a very talented artist at that."

"I have. She's my best friend." Aubrey smiled.

Charles looked at his ringing phone in his hand.

"Lexi's calling. I have to take this. I'll be right back," he spoke as he walked away.

"I take it Lexi is his wife?" she asked.

"No. She's his girlfriend. But by the way they act, they might as well be married."

Studying Aubrey, I noticed she looked down a lot, which signaled to me that she lacked confidence. Either that or she was extremely shy. That was something I would have to fix.

"Would you like to go get a drink or maybe some coffee somewhere?" I asked with the hopes she'd say yes because I really wanted to fuck her tonight.

"I'm not sure that's a good idea."

"Why not? Am I making you uncomfortable?"

"No. Not at all." She looked at me.

"Then why not?"

"Mr. Klein, I'm flattered that you would like to take me out, but I can assure you that I'm not the type of girl you're probably used to."

"Why don't you tell me what type of girl you think I'm used to?" I smirked.

"Someone who can see you," she replied.

"Excuse me?" I asked in confusion.

"I'm blind, Mr. Klein."

"What? Is that your way of telling me that you don't want to go out and have a drink? You don't have to make something like that up."

"No. I'm just telling you the truth. The painting we were talking about; the one on the wall."

"Yes. What about it?"

"Look at the name of it."

I walked over to the painting and looked at the sign that was above it. The painting was titled *Aubrey*. I was in shock and in total disbelief. She wasn't lying and I was at a loss for words. I had no clue that she was blind.

"I'm sorry. I had no idea."

"It's fine. I generally surprise people when I spring that on them." She smiled.

She had a beautiful smile. One that I couldn't seem to tear my eyes from.

"There you are. I've been looking all over for you. Penelope wants to talk to you." Some guy spoke as he lightly touched her arm.

"Ian, I would you like you to meet Ethan Klein. Ethan, this is my best friend, Ian."

"Nice to meet you, Ian."

"Likewise, Mr. Klein."

She placed her hand slightly above his elbow, and before she walked away, she spoke, "It was very nice to meet you, Mr. Klein. Enjoy the rest of your evening."

I watched as the two of them walked away. My fist involuntarily clenched itself. I turned and once again looked at the painting, recalling her words, "Even in a world of darkness, you will always see light." As I was standing there, Charles walked over to me.

"Why are you still standing here?" he asked.

"Because I'm going to buy this painting."

"Seriously? Why that one?"

"It's special."

"How?" He arched his brow at me.

"It just is."

"Good for you." He patted my back. "Now if you'll excuse me, I'm going to fetch a glass of champagne."

I looked over at the door and saw Aubrey and her friend walking out. A feeling stirred inside me. Clenching my jaw, I took in a deep breath as a woman approached me.

"I noticed you've been standing here staring at that painting. I'm Penelope, the artist who painted the portrait."

"Nice to meet you, Penelope." I extended my hand. "I'm Ethan Klein. The portrait is beautiful and I would like to buy it."

"You've made an excellent choice. This happens to be one of my favorites." She smiled.

"The girl in the painting. I just met her a little bit ago."

"You met Aubrey? She's a wonderful woman."

"She's very nice and I was hoping that you could perhaps give me her phone number. That is, if she has a phone."

Penelope laughed. "Of course she has a phone."

"She told me she was blind, so I wasn't sure."

"Just because she's blind, Mr. Klein, doesn't mean that she stopped living life. She can do more than a person who has their sight can. May I ask why you want her number?"

"I asked her out for a drink and she declined. But I don't want to accept that. I would like to get to know her better."

"Aubrey steers clear of men. She's had her heart broken, and to be honest, guys are just dicks when it comes to someone like her. If you're looking for a one-night stand or something, she's not your girl. I'm very protective of my best friend."

"I understand that, but even though she told me she was blind, it doesn't change the fact that I would like to take her out. She didn't scare me off."

She sighed. "I won't give you her number without her permission, but I will tell you something. Tomorrow is Saturday, and every Saturday morning around nine o'clock, she goes to Shakespeare Garden in Central Park to read for a while."

"By herself?" I asked as I cocked my head.

"Yes. By herself. She isn't handicapped, Mr. Klein."

"I didn't say she was." I narrowed my eye at her.

"If you want to talk to her, you'll find her there. Now, if you'll excuse me, I'll have the gallery take the painting down and wrap it up for you."

"Thank you. One more thing: please do not tell her that I purchased this painting."

Her eyebrows furrowed as she bit down on her bottom lip. "I won't and don't you be telling her that I told you where she goes on Saturdays."

"I won't. You have my word."

Chapter 4
Aubrey

Climbing out of the cab, I said goodnight to Ian, took my cane from my purse, and walked through the revolving door to my apartment building.

"Good evening, Aubrey."

"Good evening, Kale." I smiled. "How was your vacation in Mexico?"

"It was great. The wife and I had a wonderful anniversary."

"I'm happy to hear that. I want to hear all about it tomorrow. Have a good night."

"You too, Aubrey."

Taking the elevator up to the second floor, I inserted my key into the lock and stepped inside my apartment. I couldn't stop thinking about Ethan Klein and it was driving me insane. It wasn't only his scent, but it was also the sound of his voice; deep but not too deep and very smooth. He spoke words with confidence and there was a sexiness to his tone. A voice like that hadn't affected me like this in a very long time, if ever. I had to decline his invitation for a drink because I knew exactly how it would play out. I'd been there, done that, and it was something I wasn't going to allow myself to get involved in again.

Men thought I was beautiful and I got hit on all the time. Don't get me wrong; it was flattering since I didn't have a clue what I actually looked like, but it went either of two ways. Some guys told me they just wanted to sleep with me because they found it a huge turn-on that I couldn't see them and others didn't bother to call after the second date. I'd even had some guys tell me that my blindness actually freaked them out, even though they thought they'd be okay with it. They couldn't look past it and get to know the person I truly was. That was when I decided that it was in my best interest to forget men and live my life the only way I knew how. If they couldn't adapt, it was their problem, not mine. But I made it my mission and stayed away in order to protect my heart. I had my Aunt Charlotte, Ian, Penelope, and a few other friends and they were all I needed.

****

Placing my book in my bag, I grabbed my cane and coffee and climbed into the cab that I had called for before leaving my apartment.

"Hey, Aubrey."

"Hi, Jeff."

"It still amazes me each time you climb into my cab that you know it's me."

"I recognize your voice." I smiled.

"That's pretty cool. Where you off to? Shakespeare Garden?"

"Yes, please."

I had five cab drivers that I called for on a regular basis. The cab company knew me and my situation and they were always very accommodating.

"We're here, Aubrey," Jeff spoke. "Just charge it to your card?"

"Yes, please."

Reaching into my wallet, I pulled out a few dollars and handed them to him for the tip. I mostly only carried ones, fives, and tens. I had a system in place of how I told the bills apart. For everything else, I used my credit card.

"Thanks, Jeff. Have a good day."

"You too."

Climbing out of the cab, I walked into Shakespeare Garden, using my cane for guidance, and took a seat on a wooden bench that sat on a cobblestone walk lined with flowers. This was my place of peace. Not that my life was crazy by any means, but there was something about it that relaxed me.

Opening my book, I began to run my fingers along the braille lettering. As I was reading and taking in the warmth of the sun, a scent, the same scent from last night, occupied my space. I could hear soft footsteps approaching and then they suddenly stopped.

"Hello, Mr. Klein. What are you doing here?"

"How did you know it was me?"

"Your cologne." I smiled.

"Wow. You're good, Miss Callahan. I was just taking a stroll on this beautiful morning and I saw you sitting here. I couldn't believe it. I was trying to approach with caution because I didn't want to scare you."

"Do you frequently take a stroll through Shakespeare Garden on Saturday mornings? And you wouldn't have scared me. I don't scare easily."

"Sometimes I do."

"Please, have a seat." I patted the bench. "Unless you have somewhere you have to be."

"No. Nowhere in particular."

"I find it hard to believe that you just take strolls." I laughed.

"Why?" he asked.

"Because you're not the type."

"And how do you know what type of person I am?"

"I can sense it."

"Then please enlighten me."

I sighed. "Okay. You're a businessman. A powerful, very busy businessman. Work is your life and you like control. You don't have time to take strolls through Central Park, nor do you have the desire to."

"Seriously, Aubrey. How the hell do you do that?"

I couldn't help but let out a light laugh.

"Be honest with me, Ethan. What are you doing here in Shakespeare Garden?"

I heard him inhale a sharp breath. "Fine. Obviously, there's no pulling one over on you. I asked your friend, Penelope, for your number last night. She wouldn't give it to me, but she told me if I wanted to see you, this is where I'd find you this morning. But, please, do not tell her that I told you. I gave her my word."

"I won't tell her. Why did you want my number?"

"Because I want to take you out and I don't want to take no for an answer."

"Why do you want to take me out?"

"I think you're a nice girl and I'd like to get to know you."

"But why?"

"Why what?"

"Why do you want to get to know me?"

"What's with all the questions?" he asked.

"Don't answer a question with a question. You're buying time to come up with a line that will sweep me off my feet. Just so you know, I don't get swept up that easy. I may not have eyesight, but I'm not stupid."

"I never said you were, Aubrey, and I'm not trying to come up with a line. I find you attractive and to be a very nice girl."

"You don't even know me. We talked about ten minutes. Maybe twenty at the most."

"Exactly, and in that ten or twenty minutes, I felt like you were someone I wanted to get to know better. See, no pick-up line. Just a simple fact."

It was against my better judgment, but I couldn't seem to resist his charm. After all, he did come to the garden to see me.

"Okay. I will go out with you so you can get to know me better. But one time, and one time only." I smiled.

Chapter 5
Ethan

I was happy that she agreed to let me take her out. She said one time and that was fine with me. One time with her was all I needed. If it was that easy to convince her to go out with me, then it would be just as easy to get her into my bed. She was different from the other women I fucked and different was what I wanted. I was getting bored.

"Great. How about I take you to dinner tonight?"

"How about lunch?" she smirked.

"Or lunch." I laughed. "What are you reading?"

"*Pride and Prejudice* by Jane Austen."

"I see it's in braille." I leaned closer to have a better look.

"Yes. It's the only way I can read." She smiled.

God, she was so beautiful and I just wanted to reach out and touch her. I wanted to feel the softness of her long blonde hair through my fingers.

"How would you like to take a walk through the garden?" I blurted out with no control. *What the fuck just happened?*

A small smile crossed her lips. "That would be nice."

"Then let's go." I stood up and held out my hand to her like an idiot. She couldn't see it and I pulled back. This was going to take some getting used to.

Putting her book in her bag, she grabbed her cane and stood up.

"How about you use my arm instead of that cane?"

"Thank you. I appreciate that." She smiled.

She folded up her cane, placed it in her bag, and lightly placed her hand above my elbow.

"You need to walk a half a step ahead of me so I can follow your direction. And, you'll also need to tell me when we approach a curb or stairs. I'm trusting you, Mr. Klein."

"You're safe with me, Miss Callahan." I smirked.

"Why don't you ask me what you're dying to know?" she spoke as we began walking.

"How do you know what I'm thinking?"

"It's always the first question people ask the minute they meet me." She stared straight ahead.

"Have you always been blind?"

"No. It happened when I was eight years old after a horrible car crash I was in with my parents. They were killed and I lost my eyesight," she replied in a soft-spoken voice.

I felt a twinge of something in my heart. Pain perhaps? Pain for her because she lost her parents, or pain because she lost her sight. I was concerned because I didn't feel things like that.

"I'm sorry."

"Thank you. That was a long time ago."

"Who raised you?" I asked as we walked along the flower-lined path.

"My Aunt Charlotte and Uncle Lee. She was my mother's sister. They moved me here right after I got out of the hospital."

"You're not from New York?" I asked.

"No. I was born in California."

Suddenly, my phone started to ring. Pulling it from my pocket, I noticed it was Jarod calling.

"I have to take this. Excuse me for a moment." I stopped and she stopped beside me.

"Go ahead."

"You better have some news for me," I answered.

"We might. We went to your office and saw you hadn't been in. Are you coming in today?"

"I could if you had something good."

"I think we do, Mr. Klein."

"I'm on my way." I ended the call and placed my phone in my pocket. "I'm sorry, Aubrey, but that was work. I have to go into the office."

"It's fine." She smiled.

"Can we resume this later on tonight?" I asked.

"Sure. Why don't you come over for dinner? I'll cook you a nice meal."

"You cook?" I asked in confusion.

"Yes." She laughed. "Hard to believe. Isn't it?"

"No. I'm sorry. I didn't mean to—"

"No worries, Mr. Klein. I get it all the time. It's hard for people who have sight to understand."

"Let me take you home. My driver is already here."

"You have your own driver?"

"Yes. His name is Harry. That way, I'll know where you live for when I come over later."

"Thank you. I appreciate it."

We walked out of Shakespeare Garden and Harry was waiting for us with the limo door open.

"Harry, I would like you to meet Aubrey Callahan."

"Hello, Aubrey." He smiled as he held his hand out to her.

Looking at him, I mouthed and pointed to my eye. "She's blind."

"It's nice to meet you, Harry." She placed her hand in his and then slid into the backseat.

Harry shot me a look and then shut the door after I climbed in.

"We're taking Miss Callahan home first and then I need to go to the office."

"Your address, Miss Callahan?" Harry asked.

"200 East 82nd Street."

"You're an upper East Sider, eh?"

"Yes. I am. Where do you live?" she asked.

"In a townhome on West 88th Street."

"Ah. So you're an upper West Sider." She grinned.

"Do you live by yourself?" I asked out of curiosity.

"Yes. But my Aunt Charlotte lives across the hall. She owns the building. She inherited it after my uncle passed away."

"How long have you lived there?"

"About seven years. He passed away when I was eighteen."

"I'm sorry for your loss."

"Thank you."

Harry pulled up to the curb, climbed out, and opened the door for Aubrey, taking hold of her hand and helping her out.

"Thank you, Harry." She smiled.

"Which apartment are you?" I asked.

"Apartment 2B. I'll let Kale, the doorman, know you'll be arriving, say around seven o'clock?"

"Seven is fine. I'll see you then."

Harry shut the door and I watched out the window as Aubrey walked into her building. I couldn't believe she was cooking dinner for me. I would have rather gone out, but she seemed excited about it. Maybe it was better we stayed in at her place tonight. I would probably have a better chance at fucking her there.

"Really, Ethan?" Harry turned and shot me a look.

"Really what?" I narrowed my eye at him.

"A blind girl? What the hell is the matter with you? I knew something was up when you told me to drop you off at Shakespeare Garden."

"I happen to find her very attractive and she's a nice girl."

"You, my friend, have just crossed the line as far as assholes go."

"Shut up and just drive." I scowled.

Chapter 6
Aubrey

As I was opening the door to my apartment, I heard Aunt Charlotte's door across the hall open and she followed me inside.

"How was reading time?" she asked.

"I really didn't get much reading done."

"Why not?"

"Someone was there I knew and we ended up talking."

"Do I know this someone?" she asked.

"No. I just met him last night at Penelope's exhibition."

"Him?"

"Yes. His name is Ethan Klein. Apparently, he wanted my phone number last night and asked Penelope for it. She wouldn't give it to him but told him where I go on Saturday mornings."

"I'm sorry. Did you say Ethan Klein?" Her voice became serious.

"Yes. Do you know him?"

"Personally, no. I've heard of him. He's a very ruthless businessman, Aubrey, and I think it's best you stay away from him. He's a womanizer on top of it and has a whole slew of women at his beck and call. I've heard the talk around the city."

"You heard talk? Talk is talk, Aunt Charlotte. I'll decide for myself if I should stay away from him. In fact, he's coming over for dinner tonight."

"What? Oh, Aubrey, please for the love of God listen to me. I don't think that's a good idea."

"Aunt Charlotte." I sighed. "I'm twenty-five years old. I'm not a child. I can see who I want."

"I know that, dear, but I don't want you getting hurt again."

"I can protect myself. Don't worry about me."

"Well, I do. I can't help it." She walked over to me and grabbed my hand.

"I'll be fine. I promise." I smiled.

"What are you going to cook for dinner?" she asked.

"Breaded chicken, baked potatoes, fresh green beans, and salad."

"Sounds good. Mind if I join you?"

"Yes. Actually, I do mind." I laughed.

She kissed my forehead. "I'm going to go. If you need any help, call me."

"Thank you. I will."

I loved my Aunt Charlotte more than anyone in the world, but sometimes, she didn't know how to stop treating me like a child.

****

After returning home from the market down the street, I set the two bags of groceries down on the kitchen counter. When I pressed the button on my watch, it told me that it was five o'clock. I had just enough time to jump in the shower and then start prepping for dinner.

I kept thinking about what my Aunt Charlotte said about Ethan. About him being a ruthless businessman and a womanizer. I could sense that, but there was something else I sensed. I sensed a side to him that he kept hidden away. A part of himself that he didn't want anyone to know. That was why I agreed to go out with him.

After my shower, I went into the kitchen and started to prepare dinner. Once the chicken and potatoes were in the oven, I gathered all the ingredients for the salad. As I was cutting up the lettuce, there was knock on the door. My belly did a little flip, knowing that he was on the other side.

"Hello, Ethan." I smiled as I opened the door.

"Hello, Aubrey. Were you one hundred percent sure that it was me before opening the door? I didn't hear you ask who it was."

"My watch told me that it was six fifty-nine and I told you to be here at seven. So, I was pretty confident it was you. Come on in."

****

Ethan

She looked as beautiful as she did this morning in her long floral spaghetti-strap dress. The way her hair fell over shoulders with soft curls aroused me.

"You look incredible, but I'm still concerned that you didn't ask who was at the door."

She let out a light laugh. "I knew it was you. Trust me. But to put your mind at ease, I always ask."

"I hope so."

The apartment looked nice. Her living area had a light gray color on the walls that was accented with a dark gray couch, a couple of matching chairs, and a glass coffee table and end tables. The kitchen was on the small side with dark cabinets, a black granite countertop, and all stainless steel appliances. I suppose you could say that I was surprised at how nice it looked.

"It smells good in here," I spoke as I followed her into the kitchen.

"I hope you like chicken."

"I do."

I stood there and watched as she cut up some cucumbers. I was getting overly nervous that she was going to cut herself.

"Can I help you with anything?" I asked. "Maybe I can cut those cucumbers for you."

"Thanks, Ethan, but I got this. Am I making you nervous with this knife?"

"Just a bit." I chuckled.

"Don't worry. I cook all the time. I know what I'm doing. I was trained."

"Trained?"

"After the accident, my aunt sent me to Lavelle Institute for the Blind. I learned to read braille and they taught me how to live independently. I've had many years of training. So don't worry about me cutting up some cucumbers."

"I'm sorry. I didn't—"

"Don't apologize, Ethan. You have nothing to be sorry for. I've accepted a long time ago the fact that I make people a little uncomfortable. That's how the world works. People think they have to be careful around me and they don't. I'm just like everybody else. The only difference is I can't see."

"And you're probably a hell of a lot smarter than most people," I spoke.

"I don't know about that." She laughed.

She finished making the salad and took the bowl over to the table.

"Let me help with something."

"No. Just go sit down and relax. I've got this."

I sighed as I took a seat at the table and watched her pull the chicken from the oven. She inserted a thermometer in the middle and it read her the temperature.

"Perfect," she spoke as she took down two plates from the cupboard and placed a piece of chicken on each of them with a baked potato and green beans.

She stood in front of the table, holding the plates, and she spoke, "Which seat are you sitting in? Twelve o'clock, three o'clock, six o'clock, or nine o'clock?"

"Umm."

"Look at where I'm standing and pretend you're a clock."

"Twelve o'clock." I smiled.

She walked over and set the plate down perfectly in front of me while setting hers at three o'clock.

"Would you like some wine?" she asked.

"I'd love some."

"Red or white?"

"Whatever you're having."

I sat there in amazement at how flawlessly she cooked and served dinner. She set my wine glass down in front of me and then took her seat.

"What do you do all day?" I asked as I cut into my chicken.

"I read and I tutor kids online during the summer for extra income."

"Tutor kids? Tutor them in what?"

"English."

It was a good thing she couldn't see the expression on my face because I was sure she'd be offended by it.

"I don't understand."

She gave me a small smile. "I'm a teacher. I teach English Lit over at Roosevelt High School."

"In Brooklyn?" I asked.

"Yes."

"I—"

"You don't understand how a blind person could teach a class, right?"

"No. Yes. I mean—"

"It's okay, Ethan. I get that same reaction from everyone. I graduated from NYU, did my student teaching at Roosevelt, and when I graduated, they offered me a job as a full-time teacher, teaching eleventh grade. Actually, I have to report to school on Monday to get things set up and school starts on Tuesday."

"How long have you been teaching?"

"This will be my second year." She carefully picked up her wine and took a sip.

"Have you always wanted to be a teacher?"

"Ever since I was ten years old. I wanted to help others like I was helped. I was a child when I lost my sight and it was the most difficult time of my life. Trying to adapt in a world of darkness was something I didn't think I could do. But I did and I owed it all to my teachers at Lavell and my aunt and uncle. I could sense the gratification they got when they taught me something and I wanted to experience that."

"Why English Literature?"

"I fell in love with it since I was first introduced to Shakespeare. For me, it was a new way of seeing the world; their world and the time in which it was written. When I read someone like Jane Austen or Ernest Hemingway, even Shakespeare, I am so absorbed in their writing and stories that I get lost and sometimes I forget I'm blind. If that makes sense."

I sat there and stared at her as a small smile crossed my face.

"It does make sense. Roosevelt is a tough school. Not actually the school, but the kids. I'm really surprised you like teaching there."

"A lot of the students there come from broken homes and some of them are just there because they have no choice. But when they walk into my classroom, they walk into another world. They feel my passion and, after a while, they become passionate about it too. If I can help one student follow their dreams, then every day of teaching is worth it."

This woman was incredible as far as I was concerned, and the more we talked, the more intrigued I became about her. I desperately wanted to reach out and run my hand across her cheek because controlling myself in her presence was becoming difficult.

Chapter 7
Aubrey

I got up from my chair and began to clear the table. I heard Ethan get up and follow me into the kitchen, open up the dishwasher, and place his plate inside it.

"I can clean up," I spoke.

"And I can help. You cooked a wonderful meal for me and it's the least I could do."

I wanted to know about him. About his life and about his business. We only talked about me during dinner and nothing about him.

"Now that you know about me, what's your story, Mr. Klein?"

"Well, I grew up in Manhattan. I have a sister named Lila. I started my technology company when I was twenty-one years old and the rest is history."

"Come on. There's more to you than that." I smiled.

"Not really. My parents sold my childhood home about six years ago and moved to Long Island."

"Your parents must be very proud of you."

"They are."

"So that's all you're going to say?" I asked.

"That's all there is."

I had this overwhelming desire to be close to him. If he were to ask me to have sex with him, I probably would. He was mysterious and I found that to be a turn-on. Maybe because I hadn't had sex in centuries. Okay, not centuries, but it sure as hell felt like it. I needed to know what he looked like.

"How tall are you?" I asked.

"Six foot one," he replied.

"What color is your hair?"

"Brown, and my eyes are green just like yours."

I followed his voice until I was sure I was standing in front of him. Reaching out, I took hold of his hand, placed his palm face up and ran my hand across it. I heard the sound of the sharp inhale he took. Bringing my hands to his face, I ran my fingers along his jawline. It was strong and masculine with light stubble. Tracing the shape of his lips, I felt the softness of them over my fingers. My thumbs traced his perfectly straight and narrow nose and then slid across to his high cheekbones. When I moved up to his eyes, he closed them. They felt perfect. An image formed in my mind of how I saw him. Sexy, hot, desirable. I ran my fingers through his hair. It was short all the way around. Almost shaved, but not quite. My hands clasped his shoulders and ran down his arms. They were strong and muscular.

"You're killing me, Aubrey," he whispered in a soft voice.

"I'm sorry. It's the only way I can visualize what you look like."

I felt his hand on the side of my face and I was ready and all too eager for his lips to touch mine, but instead, he pulled his hand away.

"What's wrong?"

"Nothing." I heard his footsteps as he walked away.

"I'm sorry. I didn't mean to—"

In a mere second, he grabbed me and his tongue slid across my neck.

"I want you, Aubrey. I'm sorry, but I do."

"I want you too."

His tongue glided along my neck as his hands reached behind and unzipped my dress. Sliding the straps off my shoulders, he let it fall to the ground and picked me up and carried me into the bedroom.

****

Ethan

I tried to control myself, but I couldn't. There was more to her than I originally thought and I would end up hurting her. I unhooked her bra and tossed it to the side. Her breasts were round, perky, and beautiful, and her nipples were the perfect light pink color I knew they would be. Laying her down on the bed, my mouth devoured each breast and my teeth clamped around her hardened peaks. Her hands roamed through my hair as my tongue slid down her toned stomach. I needed to be inside her. Standing up, I stripped out of my clothes, tore the wrapper between my teeth, and rolled the condom over my hard cock. Reaching down, I gripped the sides of her beautiful white lace panties and slid them down. My fingers roamed up her thigh and dipped inside her. She was filled with warmth and my cock was screaming for attention. Her moans, as my finger explored her, heightened my excitement.

"Are you enjoying this?" I asked with a mere whisper.

"Yes," she replied with bated breath.

I hovered over her, my finger still inside, and took her breast in my mouth. She gasped when my thumb pressed against her clit. Her head tilted back and her moans reached their peak as her body tightened and she orgasmed. I couldn't help but smile as I watched the expression on her face.

She was ready for me and I was ready for her. Positioning myself perfectly over her, I thrust inside. She was tight and she felt so fucking good. A low rumble formed in my chest as I moved in and out of her.

"You're so tight. My God, you feel so good."

"Don't stop, Ethan," she panted as her nails dug into my back.

"I don't intend to, sweetheart."

I thrust harder and picked up the pace. Her legs were wrapped tightly around my waist as her hand reached up and softly touched my face. She was so damn beautiful and I couldn't stop staring at her lips. So full and perfectly shaped. She let out another loud moan as she came. I thrust deep inside her one last time and strained as I pushed out every last drop of come I had inside me. I lowered myself and buried my face into the side of her neck. Our hearts were beating fast and our breathing was unsteady. We lay there for a moment until I pulled out of her and headed to the bathroom.

When I returned to the bedroom, I found her sitting up and the sheet covering her naked body. I sat down on the edge of the bed and ran my finger along her jaw.

"Are you okay?" I asked.

"Yes. I'm fine." She gave a small smile.

"I suppose I should go."

"If you want to, but you can stay."

My fists clenched and, for the first time in nine years, I was torn with breaking one of my rules. Rules I didn't dare break for my protection.

"I have to be at the office early tomorrow. I have a lot of work to do before Monday morning." The back of my hand swept over her cheek.

"Okay. I understand."

I got up from the bed, grabbed my clothes from the floor, and got dressed.

"Can I get your number?" I asked as I held my phone in my hand.

"Sure." She smiled as she rattled it off.

She took her phone from the nightstand and handed it to me.

"Could you put your number in my phone? And don't forget your name or I won't know who's calling."

I let out a light laugh. "Of course."

Sitting back down on the edge of the bed, I ran my fingers down her hair.

"Thank you for dinner. I had a great time tonight."

"You're welcome. So did I."

"Good night, Aubrey. Make sure you lock the door when I leave."

"Good night, Ethan, and I will."

Walking out of her apartment building, I climbed into the limo and slammed the door.

"What happened?" Harry turned to me.

"Nothing. Just drive," I snapped.

"You better not have hurt that poor girl." He pulled away from the curb.

"I'm not too sure I didn't." I stared out the window.

Chapter 8
Aubrey

I slipped into my robe and then locked the door. I couldn't tell you what was going through my head. I was happy I slept with him, but on the other hand, I wasn't so sure I made the right decision. I got caught up in him and I didn't know sex could be that great. I never had an orgasm before during sex. But with him, I had not one, but two. I was on cloud nine, yet I was feeling a little sad. I didn't want him to leave. He touched me in a way that I had never been touched before. There was one problem; he didn't kiss me, and the fact that he could make love to me without our lips touching at least once bothered me. Bringing my hands up to my head, I took in a deep breath. Why did I have this feeling that I would never hear from him again? I crawled into bed and sank beneath the covers. Closing my eyes, I tried like hell to put him out of my mind, but I could still feel him. All of him.

I'd awoken to the sound of a knock at my front door and Penelope's voice alerting me that it was her. Stumbling out of bed, I yawned as I headed to the door and opened it.

"Aubrey, it's twelve o'clock. Did you just get up?"

"Yep. I sure did. I didn't realize what time it was. Come on in."

Shutting the door, I went to the kitchen and made a cup of coffee.

"Coffee?" I asked.

"No thanks. I already had my fill of caffeine this morning. You never sleep in this late. Are you sick?"

"No. I was up all night. You better sit down; there's something I need to tell you."

"Oh?" I heard her open the refrigerator door. "I have a feeling I'm going to need a glass of wine."

I took my coffee and sat down on the couch. Penelope took a seat next to me.

"So what happened?"

"I had sex."

"Shut up!" She placed her hand on my arm. "With who?"

"You know who."

"How would I know who you had sex with? I haven't spoken to you since Friday—OH!"

I laughed. "So you do know!"

She let out a sigh. "I didn't think you'd sleep with him so quickly. That's not like you. What happened?"

"He came to Shakespeare Garden, which I know you told him where I was, and we talked and took a walk. I invited him over for dinner and one thing led to another. I have to ask you something."

"What?"

"Is he as hot as I think he is?"

"Totally hot. Sexy as fuck, to be exact. I admit that my panties got a little wet just by looking at him."

"I figured." I smiled. "I could totally sense his hotness."

"So where is he? Did he stay the night?"

"No. He left right after we had sex. God, Penelope, I'm not sure if I made a mistake or not."

"Listen, doll. Look at it this way; you had sex for the first time, in, well, forever, and with a smoking hot man. I can assure you that he was the hottest guy you ever fucked. Don't get overly emotional over it."

"He wouldn't kiss me."

"Huh? What do you mean?"

"He wouldn't kiss me on the lips and that bothers me a little."

"Did you have an orgasm?" she bluntly asked.

"Yes. Two." I grinned.

"Then that's all that matters." She patted my hand. "Mouth kisses don't mean shit anyway."

"You think?"

"I know. Those are reserved for the guys who actually love a woman. As long as their mouths are touching all the other pleasure points on your body, then you have nothing to complain about."

I let out a light laugh and silently thought to myself how magical his mouth was all over my body.

****

Ethan

My eyes flew open and my sheets were drenched in a pool of sweat from a nightmare I hadn't had in years. I lay there, my heart pounding rapidly and a sick feeling in the pit of my stomach. I swallowed hard as I reached over and grabbed my phone. Looking at the time, it was seven a.m. I never slept that late. Granted, it was Sunday, but I was always up by six. It was that damn nightmare that had me in its grip. One I couldn't awake from just like all those years ago. The same nightmare that plagued my mind and haunted me for too long.

My feet hit the floor and I sat there, elbows on my knees with my face buried in my hands. I took in a deep breath as I stood up and went into the bathroom to take a shower. As I stood there and let the water beat down on me, I wondered why now. Why last night? After shaving and getting dressed, I headed down to the kitchen, where Ingrid, my housekeeper, was sitting at the island having a cup of coffee.

"My sheets need changing," I spoke as I grabbed a cup and poured some coffee into it.

"Good morning to you too, Ethan. I just changed your sheets yesterday. Is someone up there?" she asked as she arched her brow.

"Is anyone ever up there, Ingrid?" I snapped.

"Then why do they need changing? I think I have the right to know since I just put a fresh set on yesterday. Did you get a little too excited last night?" she asked with a cocky attitude.

"No. And what's with all the nosy questions? I pay you to clean for me, not to question me," I spoke with a harsh voice.

She got up from her stool and waved her hand in the air as she walked over to the refrigerator to put the milk away.

"I'm your housekeeper, your chef, your personal errand runner, your therapist, and your friend. What's going on, Ethan?"

She was right. She was all those things, but most importantly, she was my friend. I hired her to come work for me right after I started my company and moved into this townhouse. I placed an ad online giving very strict instructions as to what I was looking for. She answered my ad and only came for the interview to tell me off. Apparently, she didn't like me. The one thing about Ingrid was that she didn't have a filter. She was fifty years old, stood about five foot five, full figure, long black hair that she always wore in a bun, and brown eyes. She was wise and I could talk to her as if I'd known her my whole life. The good thing with us was that she put up with me and I put up with her. But I did pay her very well for putting up with my demands and my attitude ninety percent of the time.

I sighed as I took a seat at the table and she pulled out the eggs from the refrigerator.

"I had that nightmare last night."

Just as she was about to crack the egg, she stopped and looked at me.

"Why? It's been years."

"I know and I don't know why." I took a sip of coffee.

"What did you do last night?" She cracked three eggs in a bowl.

"Had dinner with a woman I met the other night at her apartment."

She rolled her eyes as she poured the eggs into the hot pan.

"Well, that's no different from any other night."

I wasn't ready to discuss Aubrey with her, if I was even going to mention her at all. I didn't need to hear her comments and backlash like I did from Harry. I got what I craved and desired from her and now it was over.

Chapter 9
Aubrey

No matter how busy I kept myself the past couple of days, I couldn't stop thinking about Ethan. He had my phone number, yet I hadn't heard from him. Ian told me that guys will typically wait a couple of days before calling a girl they went on a date with because they didn't want to seem too eager. Penelope told me that he was nothing but a man whore, he would probably never call, and to put him out of my mind and move on. I tried. I really did, but he wasn't so easy to forget.

"Hi, Aubrey," I heard Gigi's voice speak as I walked into my classroom.

"Hi, Gigi." I smiled as she walked over and gave me a hug. "How was Italy?"

"Amazing."

Gigi Graham was my teaching assistant and had been with me since my first day as a teacher last year. She had attended college with the hopes of becoming a teacher herself until she became ill and had to drop out. She was a thirty-year-old woman who married her high school sweetheart and didn't need to work. But she loved being in a classroom, so she decided to become a teaching assistant instead of going back to college and finishing her degree.

I ran my hand along the steel edge of my desk and smiled as I sat down in my chair. It felt really good to be back. The first bell of the morning rang and the students started to shuffle in. Once everyone found a seat, Gigi closed the door. Getting up from my chair, I picked up a white piece of paper with squares on it and placed it on the first desk closest to the door.

"Good morning, everyone." I smiled. "I'm Miss Callahan, but you can call me Aubrey. I don't believe in formalities at your age. We're all adults here, right?" I grinned. "I call you by your first name, so in turn, you should call me by mine. Welcome to English Literature. As some of you may know, I am blind. For those of you who didn't, surprise. I would like to introduce you to my teaching assistant, Gigi Graham. She will be here every day in class with us, making sure you are on your best behavior. I can promise you that by the time the school year ends, we will be like a family, and that's something I take very seriously. Just to give you a little background information about me, I lost my parents in a horrible car accident when I was eight years old, the same accident that took my sight. I was angry, depressed, and felt like there was no hope for me, like I'm sure some of you are feeling right at this very moment. But I fought back, I won, and here I am today teaching you beautiful men and women all about English Literature. The point to this story is no matter how bad life seems right now, you can and will conquer it, but you, and only you have to put in the effort. Now." I smiled. "The seats you are sitting in will be the seats you will sit in for the rest of the school year, and I will know if you decide to be funny and switch."

The subtle laugh of the students filled the room.

"I don't really have any rules. I just ask that you be respectful, not only to me or Gigi, but to your classmates as well. If you want to bring in snacks or a drink, feel free, but be prepared to share with your teacher." I smiled.

I repeated the same speech for the next five classes and before I knew it, the first school day of the new year had come to an end. As I was putting my laptop in my bag, Ian walked into the room.

"How was your first day?" he asked.

"It was great. How was yours?"

"Good. I actually had some students excited to learn about history and the rest of them just slept."

I laughed.

Ian was hired as a teacher shortly after I was. He started off as a substitute for one of the history teachers who went on maternity leave. She never came back and the students really liked him, so the school offered him the job. We drove in together every day. He picked me up at my apartment in the morning and then drove me home after school let out.

"Have you heard from him yet?" Ian asked.

"No, and to be honest, I don't think I will." I threw my bag over my shoulder.

"It's probably for the best, Aubrey. From what I hear, he's bad news. You know my friend, Lance?"

"Yeah," I spoke as I placed my hand on his elbow and we walked to his car.

"He told me that his girlfriend, Amber, works at Ethan's company and he's a total dick to everyone there. He's rude, disrespectful to all his employees, and very demanding. He doesn't give a shit about anyone. They call him The Iceman."

I let out a light laugh as I climbed into Ian's Honda Accord.

"Why would they call him that?"

"Because he doesn't show any emotion or feelings toward anyone. He's as cold as ice. Amber also told him that Ethan has never been in a relationship and he uses women for sex and then drops them like a hot potato. Gee, maybe I shouldn't have told you that last part."

"It's fine, Ian. You wouldn't be my friend if you didn't. Listen, I don't expect to hear from him again, so don't worry about me."

"I guess the good thing is you had sex for the first time in forever." He grabbed my hand and gently squeezed it.

"Yeah. At least I had that." I softly smiled.

Ian dropped me off in front of my apartment building and headed home. I wouldn't lie and say that our little conversation about Ethan Klein didn't hurt a bit, because it did. But this was something I had grown used to.

****

Ethan

"Lucy!" I shouted from my office. "Where the hell is that report I asked you to finish over an hour ago?!"

"Lucy isn't at her desk and you, my friend, need to calm the fuck down," Charles spoke as he strolled into my office and took a seat across from me.

"Here's your report, sir. I was in the storage room getting new ink for the printer."

"I asked for this over an hour ago." I grabbed it from her hands.

"I'm sorry, but I—"

"I don't want to hear your sorry-ass excuses. The next time I ask for something, you better fucking get it to me when I ask for it. Do you understand me?"

"Yes, sir. Is that all?"

"Yes. Get out of my office."

I threw the report down and leaned back in my chair, taking in a long deep breath as I looked at Charles.

"What has your feathers all riled up today?" He smirked.

"Nothing. I just want things when I ask for them."

"I haven't heard from you since the art exhibition. Which, by the way, the painting was a huge success. Lexi loved it and gave me not one, but two blowjobs when she came back." He grinned.

I hadn't told Charles anything about Aubrey. The only thing he knew was that I was talking to her that night. He didn't even know that she was the girl in the painting.

"How did things go with that girl you were talking to at the gallery? What was her name again?"

"Aubrey."

"Yeah, Aubrey. You seemed to be into her."

"She invited me over to her house on Saturday for dinner."

"Way to go, Mr. Casanova. Did you fuck her? Wait, don't answer that. Of course you did."

I turned my chair sideways and stared out the window.

"Was she really bad or something?" he asked with a serious tone.

"No. She was great. She's blind."

"What?" He laughed. "Blind to the fact that you're an asshole?"

I shot him a look as I turned my chair around and faced him.

"She's blind."

He cocked his head and narrowed his eyes at me.

"Blind? As in see can't see anything, blind?"

"Yes."

"What the fuck, Ethan? Damn. That's a new one for you. You fucked a blind chick. Holy shit! How was it? Come on, tell me. Was it different? Did you get off fast knowing that she couldn't see you?"

"Knock it off, Charles!" I shouted.

"Bro, relax." He put his hands up.

"She's a great girl who has endured a lot. She wasn't born blind. She lost her sight and her parents in a car accident when she was eight. She basically had to learn to live all over again."

"Okay. So have you talked to her since?"

"No and I don't plan to. It was one night. She's no different from any of the other women I sleep with."

"Is that so? Because you just defended her and you've never done that."

"I didn't defend her."

"You did. You didn't like what I said and you jumped to her defense."

"Well, I didn't mean to."

He sighed as he got up from his chair.

"Anyway, I just stopped by to say hi since I hadn't heard from you in a few days. Oh, and by the way, I'm having a little birthday get together for Lexi on Saturday at the house. You will be there." He pointed at me.

"I wouldn't miss it."

"I'll talk to you later. Try to stay off your secretary's ass."

"Don't tell me how to run my company." I smirked.

As I picked up the report from my desk, my phone rang and it was my mother calling.

"Hello."

"Ethan, it's been ages since we heard from you."

"Sorry, Mom. I've been really busy."

"You need to come to dinner on Sunday at the house. We're celebrating Labor Day a day early."

"Okay. What time?"

"Four o'clock. Your sister and Kenny will be here too."

"I'll be there."

"Good. Do me a favor and pick up a lemon cake at that bakery I love so much."

I sighed. "Got it. One lemon cake."

"See you Sunday, Ethan."

"See you then, Mom."

As much as I loved my family, I hated going over there. My mom and dad were always on my ass about finding a nice girl, settling down, and giving them grandkids. I flat out told them the last time I saw them that they'd have to get their grandkids from Lila, my sister, because there was no way in hell I was ever having kids. Not to mention settling down with a nice girl. I didn't see them as often as I should because it was best that I stayed away. They didn't know the full story of what happened that night. They only knew what I chose to tell them.

Chapter 10

Aubrey

It was already Friday, and as I was packing up my bag to head home, my phone rang, alerting me that Penelope was calling.

"Hello."

"Tell me you don't have plans for tomorrow."

"Not really. Why?"

"Good. Then you're coming with me to a birthday party."

"Whose party?" I asked as Ian took my bag from me.

"A client's girlfriend. He contacted me and bought another one of my paintings. His girlfriend loved the one he bought at my exhibition so much that she wanted another. He said that she would love to meet me and invited me and a friend to her birthday party tomorrow. Don't make me go alone," she whined.

I let out a light laugh. "Fine. I'll go. What time does it start?"

"Five o'clock."

"Okay. I'll be ready."

"Thanks, love. I owe you."

"What are you doing right now?" I asked.

"Not much. Why?"

"Good. You can meet me and Ian at Roof on South Park in about twenty minutes and buy me a drink or two."

"Sounds good. I'll meet you both there."

****

Ethan

With a bouquet of flowers in my hand, I stepped inside Charles' and Lexi's townhome.

"Hey, Ethan." Charles smiled as he shook my hand. "Aw, you shouldn't have." He winked as he looked at the flowers.

"Very funny. Where's Lexi?"

"Outside talking to one of her friends. Follow me."

I followed him out to the patio and gave Lexi a kiss on the cheek.

"Happy birthday, Lexi." I handed her the flowers.

"Thank you, Ethan. These are beautiful. I'm going to go put them in a vase." She smiled as she walked away.

"How about a scotch?" Charles asked.

"Sounds good."

I followed him to the bar that sat in the corner of the patio.

"Scotch on the rocks for my best friend here," he spoke to the bartender.

"Wow. You went all out for this party." I smirked.

"That's because she's worth it."

The bartender handed me my drink and Charles pulled me over around the corner and reached into his pocket.

"What do you think? I just picked it up yesterday." He smiled as he held a diamond ring in the palm of his hand.

"Very nice. When are you asking her?"

"Tonight. In front of everyone."

"I thought you were going to wait until your trip to Aruba?"

"I was, but I can't wait any longer."

"I thought that was the reason you booked the trip."

"It was and I know she'll be expecting it then. So this will be more of a surprise." He grinned.

I placed my hand on his shoulder. "Congrats, bro. I'm happy for you."

"Don't congratulate me yet. She hasn't said yes."

"She will." I smiled as we walked back to the party.

I finished off my scotch and went to the bar for another. As the bartender was pouring it, I looked around. My heart stopped when I saw Aubrey standing next to Penelope, talking to Charles and Lexi. What the hell was she doing here? Shit. The bartender handed me my drink and I stood there, leaning against the bar sipping it while I stared at her. She was too damn beautiful and I didn't know what to say to her. This shouldn't have been a problem. I'd run into women all the time that I had one-night stands with. They'd yell at me or call me names and I'd just smile and keep on walking. But with Aubrey, it felt different. That was something I felt I couldn't do. I didn't want her to know I was here, so I would quietly escape and she'd never know. Not until Charles opened his big mouth.

"Ethan, look who's here!" he shouted from across the way.

Asshole.

Aubrey looked straight at me. It was as if she could see me standing there. I finished off my second scotch and casually walked over to where they were standing.

"Hello, Mr. Klein." Penelope glared at me.

"Penelope. Nice to see you again." I nodded. "Hello, Aubrey."

"Hello, Ethan," she spoke in a soft voice.

"Come on, Penelope. Come with me and Lexi and we'll show you where we hung your spectacular painting that I bought last week."

Dick.

Penelope placed her hand on Aubrey's arm.

"I'll be right back."

"Okay." She looked down and gave a small smile. "How have you been, Ethan?" she surprisingly asked.

"Busy. How about you?"

"Busy as well."

Fuck. My conscience was getting the best of me and I didn't know why and I didn't know how to control it.

"Listen, Aubrey. I'm sorry that—"

She put her hand up.

"Don't apologize, Ethan. It was one night. That's all. I didn't expect you to call."

"I wanted to, but with work and everything, I just didn't have the chance."

"It's fine. Like I said, I didn't expect a call."

"So, how's school?" I asked to make the moment less awkward.

"School is great. I have wonderful students."

"That's good." I placed my hand in my pocket. "It looks like they're starting to serve dinner. I should get—"

Before I could finish my sentence and was getting ready to make my exit, Lexi walked over and grabbed my and Aubrey's hands.

"Come on, you two. You're sitting at our table for dinner." She smiled.

"I really need to get going, Lex. I have a lot of work to do."

"Nonsense. It's my birthday and you're staying. Work can wait until tomorrow. Oh, there's someone that just showed up that I need to say hello to. Take Aubrey to that table right over there." She pointed as she walked away.

I sighed.

"It's okay, Ethan. You don't need to walk me to the table. You didn't ask to be my eyes." The corners of her mouth slightly turned upwards.

She may have been smiling on the outside, but on the inside, she was sad. I could tell. It was in the tone of her voice when she spoke those words.

"Don't be silly, Aubrey. I want to escort you to the table and, if you'll have me, I would like to sit next to you. So come on and let me escort you."

"And what if I told you that I didn't want you to sit next to me?" She lightly touched my elbow.

I chuckled. "Then I guess I'd have to find another seat."

I led her to the table, pulled out the chair, and then took the seat next to hers.

"I'm sorry if you disapprove, but I'm sitting next to you anyway. Can I let you in on a little secret?" I leaned over and whispered in her ear.

"Sure." She smiled.

"Charles is going to ask Lexi to marry him tonight."

The smile on her face grew wide as she leaned closer to me.

"I hope she says yes. It's a good thing you're staying. He may need you for support if things don't go his way."

I chuckled. "You're right."

Penelope took a seat next to Aubrey but not before shooting me a nasty look. It was obvious that she meant what she said about protecting her best friend. Charles and Lexi joined us with a couple of other friends and as soon as dinner was served, I noticed something Penelope did with Aubrey's plate. She turned it.

"Chicken is at twelve o'clock, au gratin potatoes are at three o'clock, and roasted green beans are at nine o'clock."

"Thank you," Aubrey spoke in a soft voice as she took her napkin and placed it in her lap.

"May I get you something to drink?" I asked her.

"A glass of wine would be nice. Thank you."

"I'll be right back."

Getting up from my seat, I motioned for Charles to follow me to the bar.

"What?" he asked.

"You didn't tell me that Aubrey was going to be here," I spoke with irritation.

"I didn't know. I told Penelope to bring a friend. To be honest, I forgot Aubrey was her friend. I don't understand what your problem is."

"You know I slept with her and never called her. Seeing her here makes things awkward." I grabbed the glass of wine the bartender set down.

He stood there and stared at me for a moment as his left eye narrowed.

"You see women all the time you sleep with and never call again. Why is Aubrey different?"

"She's not."

"Bullshit, Ethan. If she wasn't, you wouldn't have asked me about her being here. It's obvious that it bothers you."

"Forget I said anything." I walked back to the table. "Here's your wine." I took hold of Aubrey's hand and placed the glass in it.

"Thank you."

Touching her again brought back the memories of our night together. Her soft and silky skin, the way her perfectly manicured nails dug into my back as I thrust in and out of her, causing a sensation that was too much to bear. The way her hair lay over her shoulders and the soft and subtle moans of pleasure that escaped her lips. Lips that I desperately wanted to kiss for some reason.

I came back to reality and began eating my dinner. Small talk around the table was made, mostly by Charles asking Aubrey about her life, which was none of his damn business.

Chapter 11
Aubrey

I didn't know that Ethan would be here or else I wouldn't have come. Penelope never did tell me whose party it was and I didn't ask. If she would have told me Charles, I would have known that there would have been a ninety-nine percent chance that Ethan would have been here. It was awkward. I won't lie. Hearing his voice and smelling his scent sent my pheromones into overdrive once again. He was nervous. That much I could tell.

"I need to use the restroom," I softly spoke to Penelope.

"I'll show you where it is," Ethan spoke as he lightly grabbed hold of my hand, which was resting on the table.

Electrifying shocks traveled throughout my body at his mere touch. I swallowed hard as we both got up from our seats. He placed my arm in his and led me inside the house.

"Here you are," he spoke. "The toilet is on the left."

"Thanks, Ethan."

"You're welcome. I'll be waiting outside the door."

As soon as I finished, I washed my hands and felt around for a towel. Once I dried them off, I opened the door and his scent pelted me in the face. An ache formed between my legs as I placed my hand on his elbow. As soon as we made our way back out to the patio, we heard Charles starting to propose to Lexi. I couldn't help but smile when she screamed yes.

"I'll be damned," Ethan spoke. "She said yes."

"I knew she would."

"Shall we go congratulate them?" he asked.

"Let's." I grinned.

After congratulations and hugs were given, Ethan escorted me back to the table where the servers were just starting to serve cake.

"It's chocolate," Ethan spoke.

"Chocolate's my favorite."

"Mine too."

"Can you describe my piece to me, please?" I asked.

"Of course. It's chocolate cake with white icing and there's two pink roses on the side of your piece."

Picking up my fork, I smiled as I stuck it into the cake and took a bite.

"Oh my gosh. This is so good."

"It's very good," he spoke.

"The one thing you should know about me is that I'm a huge sweets eater. I love all kinds of pastries." I smiled.

"I do too. My housekeeper, Ingrid, makes the most amazing tarts."

"What kind does she make?" I asked as I finished off my cake.

"All kinds. Lemon, chocolate, strawberry, cherry. You name it, she makes it."

All of a sudden, I felt the soft touch of his finger against the corner of my mouth.

"You had some frosting there," he spoke.

"Thank you." I brought my napkin up to my mouth.

"Would you like to finish the walk we didn't get to take last Saturday?" he asked.

"Now?"

"Yes. Now. I'm going to my parents' house tomorrow for dinner and my mom wants me to pick up a lemon cake from this bakery she loves in SoHo. I thought maybe you could come with me to pick it up and then we can go for a walk."

"Isn't the bakery closed already?"

"Not this one." He sighed. "They're open until midnight."

"Wow, really? That's weird."

"I know."

Do I or don't I? I had just started to put Ethan Klein behind me. But there was something about him I couldn't resist and I wanted to spend time with him, even though I knew in the end he'd break my heart.

"Sure. Sounds like fun. I'll have to tell Penelope."

"Tell Penelope what?" She walked up from behind and wrapped her arms around my neck.

"I'm going to leave with Ethan if that's okay with you."

There was a moment of silence because I knew she didn't approve.

"And where do you two think you're going?"

"To a bakery to pick up a cake and then for a walk."

"Fine. Go on. Lexi asked me if I could stay a little longer because she wants to talk to me about painting her a portrait." She kissed my cheek. "You, Mr. Klein, better watch out for her."

"I will, Penelope. You don't have to worry about that."

I sighed as I got up from my seat, grabbed my purse, and held on to Ethan's elbow.

"Don't mind her; she's been very protective of me since the first day I literally ran into her and knocked all her books out of her hand."

"I don't blame her. She's your best friend and best friends look out for each other."

Ethan walked me to the limo and opened the door for me.

"It's nice to see you again, Aubrey," Harry spoke.

"It's nice to see you too."

Ethan shut the door and climbed in on the other side.

"To LuLu's bakery in SoHo, Harry."

"Let me guess. A lemon cake for Mrs. Klein?"

"Yep." He sighed.

I couldn't help but let out a light laugh. Being with him tonight was nice and I was happy that I agreed to go with Penelope to the party. A part of me was still a little mad at him for not calling me, but the other part of me was happy to be with him. I still needed to be careful where he was concerned. My heart was okay and I wanted it to stay that way. I wasn't entirely sure how he felt about me being visually impaired and I wasn't about to let myself become too involved with a man like him. He was very complicated and I needed to find out more about him. That was a strategy I needed to play out very carefully.

The limo came to a stop and Ethan announced that we had arrived at our destination. Getting out of the car, he opened the door for me.

"Take my hand so I can help you out," he spoke.

Placing my hand in his, I climbed out and then took hold of his elbow as he led me into the bakery. The minute he opened the door, the aroma of freshly baked pastries swept across my face.

"It smells so good in here." I smiled.

"It always does."

"Hello, Mr. Klein," a man spoke.

"Hello, Thaddeus. Please tell me you have a lemon cake for my mother."

"You're in luck. I have one left."

"Thank God. She would not be happy if I showed up empty handed tomorrow."

Thaddeus laughed. "Can I get you anything else?"

"Do you see anything you'd like?" Ethan asked. "Shit. I'm sorry, Aubrey."

"It's okay. Just tell me what they have."

"Donuts, cupcakes, cookies, cream puffs, slices of pie, eclairs, cheesecake."

"What kind of donuts do they have?"

"Glazed, chocolate frosted, vanilla frosted, strawberry frosted, cream filled, custard, fruit filled."

"Vanilla frosted is my favorite." I smiled.

"Give me two vanilla frosted, Thaddeus," he spoke.

"Coming right up. How about two coffees on me to go with those donuts?"

"Do you want coffee?" Ethan asked.

"Sure, but only if you're having one."

"You heard the lady. Two coffees."

Ethan handed me a bag.

"You can hold the donuts while I carry the coffees. There are some tables outside we can sit down at. Thaddeus, I'll be back in to pick up the cake when we're finished."

"I'll have it waiting for you, Mr. Klein. Enjoy your donuts and coffee."

I held on to his elbow as he led me outside.

"Hold on a second," he spoke. "Let me set these coffees down."

After setting the cups down, he took my hand and placed it on the back of a wrought-iron chair and then took the bag with the donuts in it from me.

"Here you go. I set your donut on a napkin in front of you and your coffee is to the right."

"Thank you, sir." I grinned as I reached for my donut.

"I have a question for you. It's something that I've been meaning to ask you."

"What's up?"

"The night we met, in front of the painting, did you know that painting was there?"

I couldn't help but let out a light laugh.

"No. That's why I asked you what you saw when you looked at it."

Ethan chuckled. "Ah. Okay."

Chapter 12
Ethan

I felt comfortable with her, and to be honest, I had no idea why I asked her to come with me to pick up the cake and go for a walk. A few hours ago, I was ready to leave the party unnoticed, without a trace, so she'd never know I was there. But now, a part of me was happy that I didn't because I enjoyed her company.

"Shall we take our walk now?" I asked.

"Yes. Don't forget the cake." She smiled.

"You wait here and I'll run in and grab it and give it to Harry."

When I walked back inside the bakery, Thaddeus handed me the box and I brought it outside to the limo.

"Aubrey and I are going to take a walk around SoHo for a bit." I handed him the cake.

He glared at me for a moment as he took it from my hands.

"Just call me when you're ready to leave," he spoke.

Walking back to the table, I lightly placed my hand on Aubrey's shoulder.

"Are you ready?"

"I am." She got up from her seat and took hold of my elbow.

I grabbed her hand and wrapped it around my arm, bringing her to my side.

"Will this work?" I asked.

The corners of her mouth gave way to a small beautiful smile. "Yes. This will work, but I'm also going to use my cane if that's okay with you."

"Of course it is. Why would you even ask?"

"Because people tend to feel uncomfortable. I actually had a man once tell me not to use my cane when we were on a date because he didn't want people to know that I was blind."

"You're kidding me, right?"

"No. I'm not."

"I sure hope you never saw him again after that."

"I didn't. But I did make sure to trip him a couple of times with my cane before telling him never to call me again."

I chuckled. "Good for you."

The feeling that resided inside me as her arm was wrapped around mine was something I hadn't felt in years. Something I never allowed myself to feel. I never would have walked like this if she wasn't blind and needed assistance. I didn't do this. I didn't go on walks and I certainly didn't let women wrap their arm around me. Not even in the bedroom. I was drawn to her for some reason. I tried to stay away and was successful until I saw her tonight. What is it they say? Out of sight, out of mind? She might have been out of my sight, but she certainly was never out of my mind.

"If you don't mind me asking, how do you get around?"

"Since I don't have a fancy car with a fancy driver," she smiled, "I take a cab, the subway, or I walk. Just like all the other people in New York. I also use my iPhone for almost everything, even my clothes. I used to tag each color a different way, but now I use an app and all I have to do is swish my phone over what I'm thinking about wearing and it tells me the color. It's so much easier." She laughed.

"I bet it is."

"I do have apps for almost everything. I use the GPS like it's my eyes and I use an app that tells me what's around me, like the locations of ATMs, shops, and restaurants. Technology has come so far in helping those who can't see that sometimes I fear people will become too dependent on it and then what happens if something goes wrong and we can't access that technology? That's why I still use what I've learned as well. No matter what happens, you can never lose that."

As we were walking, Aubrey's phone went off.

"It's my apartment building. Why would they be calling?"

"You better answer it."

"Hello. What? Oh my God! Was anyone hurt? How bad is it? Did you call my Aunt Charlotte? Thank you for calling."

"What happened?"

"That was Rebecca, the building manager. There was a fire in my building and everyone has been evacuated. I need to get there, Ethan."

"We'll go. Let me call Harry to bring the car around."

"Okay. I'm going to call my aunt."

I placed the call to Harry and as soon as he pulled up to the curb, we climbed in and headed straight to Aubrey's apartment building.

"Was your aunt home when it happened?" I asked after she hung up with her.

"No. She's in North Carolina visiting a friend of hers whose husband just passed away. The funeral is tomorrow and she's catching the first flight out after that."

Harry needed to park around the corner because lines of fire trucks and police cars had the street blocked. Climbing out, I grabbed on to Aubrey's hand and we headed towards the building but were shortly stopped by a police officer.

"I'm sorry, but you can't go near there."

"I live in that building," Aubrey spoke.

"I'm sorry, miss. All residents have been evacuated and need to make other arrangements for tonight."

"But—"

"Come on, Aubrey." I placed my arm around her. "Let's go back to the limo and figure this out."

"I need to call Penelope," she spoke as she climbed inside and pulled out her phone. "She didn't answer, so I'm going to try Ian." She placed her phone in her lap after she got Ian's voicemail.

I tightly clenched my fist as I looked up and saw Harry staring at me through the rearview mirror. I had my room at the Plaza she could stay at for as long as she needed, but if I sent her there, she'd be all alone and I wasn't sure that was a good idea.

"You can stay at my place tonight."

"That's sweet of you, Ethan, but I don't want to be a bother. I can get a room at a hotel nearby."

"You could, but I would feel better if you stayed at my place. Your building just had a fire and I don't think you should be alone."

"I'll be fine, Ethan. Really."

"Maybe you would be, but you're staying at my townhome tonight and I don't want to hear another word about it. Do you understand?" I spoke in an authoritative tone.

"If you insist."

"I do. Harry, take us home."

"Very well, sir." He smiled at me.

I rolled my eyes and looked out the window.

"Do you have an extra toothbrush?" She smirked.

"No. Do we need to stop at the drug store on the way?"

"I think so." She scrunched up her nose in the cutest way possible.

"Harry, we're making a stop at the drugstore."

He pulled over to the curb, and after climbing out, Aubrey held on to my arm and I walked her down the street to CVS. Walking in the store, I looked up at the signs to see which aisle the toothbrushes were in.

"Aisle five is where we need to go."

"Okay. Lead the way."

A smile crossed my lips after she said that and I couldn't help but stare at her.

"What kind of toothbrush do you want?" I asked.

"Anything medium is fine."

"Do you have a favorite color? Shit. I'm sorry."

"What are you apologizing for?"

"Asking you if you had a favorite color. I mean, without your eyesight, I would assume you don't even know what colors are."

"Hmm." She placed her finger on her lips. "I lost my eyesight when I was eight, but I learned all of my colors when I was about four years old. I know what colors are and what they look like. And to answer your question, my favorite color is blue."

"Again, I'm sorry. I wasn't thinking."

"Stop apologizing and just grab me a blue toothbrush." She laughed.

I grabbed one and asked her if there was anything else she needed.

"Do you have toothpaste?" she asked.

"Of course I do. Do you think that I never brush my teeth?"

She smiled. "Just making sure, Mr. Klein. I should also get some new deodorant. I'm almost out anyway."

"Okay. That's in the next aisle over."

She took hold of my arm and I led her to aisle four.

"What kind?"

"Secret. But make sure it's the solid, not the gel."

"Damn. Why are there so many scents?"

"Because we women have to smell nice and we always have to have options. You pick."

"Me?" I asked.

"Yes, you." Her smile grew wide.

I sighed as I started taking the caps off different scents and smelling them. What the hell was I doing?

"This lavender one smells good." I held it up to her nose.

"Lavender is my favorite scent. It's the same one I have at home."

"Lavender it is, then. Anything else?"

"I'll need some makeup remover wipes."

"Where would those be?" I asked.

"Skincare aisle?" she asked.

Looking up at the signs above, I found that skincare was one aisle over.

"Next one over. Take my arm."

I led Aubrey over to where the facial products were and picked up a package that said "Makeup Remover Cleansing Cloths," and placed it in her hand.

"What brand are they?"

Looking at the package, I spoke, "Neutrogena."

"Those are fine. Thank you."

"Anything else?"

"Nope. That should be all."

She took hold of my arm and we walked up to the cash register to check out. Once the clerk rang up Aubrey's items and gave her the total, she reached in her purse and took out her credit card, handing it to the young girl.

"You need to swipe it yourself," the clerk spoke.

"And you can't do it for her, why?" I spoke in irritation.

"Because we have the machine right there, sir."

"Ethan, it's fine," Aubrey spoke as she felt the machine with her hand.

"She's visually impaired. There's no reason why you can't do it for her."

Aubrey slid her card through the machine and the clerk shot me a look.

"Looks like she did just fine to me," she spoke with an attitude.

"You need an attitude adjustment. I want to speak with your manager."

Aubrey placed her hand on my arm. "Don't, Ethan. It's not worth it. Let's just go home."

"No. It's not okay. When you're working with the public, you don't treat customers like that."

"Thank you." Aubrey smiled at the young sales clerk. "Have a nice night."

She grabbed hold of my arm and started pulling me along. Once we climbed into the limo, Aubrey sighed.

"Listen, Ethan. I know this is new to you, but I can manage things on my own. I've lived with this for the past seventeen years. I'm used to people being rude and having attitudes."

"What did he do?" Harry asked as he looked at me through the rearview mirror with a grin.

"He was ready to get someone fired because she wouldn't slide my card for me."

"Is that so?" His glare intensified.

"She was rude and it was uncalled for," I spoke.

"She wasn't that rude and she didn't know I was blind. If I would have insisted that I couldn't do it, she would have helped me."

"Doubt it. She was a snotty little bitch."

Aubrey let out a light laugh.

As soon as Harry pulled up to the curb, I got out and opened the door for Aubrey, reaching for her hand and helping her out.

"There's two steps going up and then there's a slight turn to the left with another seven stairs leading up to the front door."

"Sounds nice." She smiled.

As we stepped inside, Aubrey spoke, "I just need you to explain to me the layout of the house."

"Oh. Well, it's eight thousand square feet with six floors."

The corners of her mouth curved upwards as a small laugh escaped her lips.

"Eight thousand square feet? Why do you, a single man, need a house this big? Are you planning on having a large family?"

"No. No family for me, ever. But, it's nice to have the room when I host parties or when my parents come to visit. Plus, it was a foreclosure and I got a good deal on it."

I led her to the right, placing her hand on the steel elevator doors.

"This is the elevator that goes to all floors and the button is right here on the left. The door opens to the right."

I pushed the button and the door opened. Aubrey walked inside and I followed, taking her hand once again and placing it on the panel on the right.

“Here are the buttons and there’s also braille lettering, which I never noticed before.”

“Most people don’t,” she spoke. “You also have stairs, right?”

“Yes. There are staircases on every floor of the house. Since we came through the front door, we are on what’s called the Parlor level, which consists of my office, the living room, and a bathroom. Since you’ll only be here one night, let me take you to your room and we can start from there.”

“Okay.” She smiled.

We stepped onto the elevator and I pushed the button to the third floor. When the doors opened, I guided Aubrey to the right.

“Your bedroom is to the right when you step out of the elevator.”

I watched as she counted the steps into the bedroom. Looking at the bed, I wanted nothing more than to throw her on it and fuck her right here and now. She had my attention all night and I wanted more.

“The bed is to the left.” I guided her over to it. “And next to it is a nightstand on each side. Across from the bed is a dresser with a TV mounted on the wall directly above it.”

“And the bathroom?” she asked.

“This way.” I placed my hand on hers, which was wrapped securely around my arm, and led her to the bathroom. “There’s a large sunken tub with jets if you want to take a bath and a glass enclosed shower next to it. Now, I’ll show you where the kitchen is.”

As soon as we made it to the kitchen, I explained the layout to her and showed her to the island, where she ran her hand along the top of the high wooden chairs.

"Describe the kitchen to me. Like the color of the wall, cabinets, and appliances."

"The walls are an eggshell color. The cabinets are a dark cherry, the granite countertops are a burgundy color and all of my appliances are stainless steel."

"I can picture it in my head and it looks beautiful." She grinned. "Which floor is your bedroom on?"

"The entire fourth floor is the master suite."

"Wow." She smirked. "Fancy having a whole floor to yourself."

"I will admit that I like it." I grinned.

Chapter 13
Aubrey

His scent filtered throughout the house. There was no escaping it. It had been a long night and I was growing tired, so I decided that I wanted to take a bath.

"If it's okay with you, I'm going to take a bath."

"That's fine. Do you need help?"

A smile escaped my lips as I lowered my head.

"I can manage on my own like I always do."

"Okay. Do you need me to help you upstairs?" he asked.

"I can find my way," I spoke as I headed towards the elevator. "Do you by any chance have any bubble bath?" I bit down on my bottom lip.

"As a matter of fact, I do. It's in the corner of the bathtub by the faucet. Ingrid put a bottle of it there since it's the guest bathroom. She said you never know when the mood would strike for a bubble bath."

"Great. Thank you."

Stepping into the bathroom, I started the water and felt around for the bottle of bubbles. Once I had it in my hand, I removed the cap and held it up to my nose, taking in the fruity scent. I undressed and carefully climbed into the bubbly water. Sinking down and closing my eyes to relax, I heard a knock on the bathroom door.

"I'm leaving a t-shirt on the bed for you to sleep in."

"Thanks, Ethan. I appreciate it."

"I'll be downstairs in my office if you need anything."

"Okay."

I inhaled deeply, letting the fruity scent of the bubbles sedate me. He was being so nice and it was hard to imagine that people called him "The Iceman." I had yet to see that side of him. Climbing out the tub, I reached for the towel, wrapped it around me, stood in front of the sink, and removed my makeup with a cleansing cloth. Once I was finished, I went to the bedroom, walked over to the bed, and picked up the cotton t-shirt that Ethan had left me. As I slipped it over my head, my phone rang and alerted me that Penelope was calling.

"It's about time you returned my call," I answered.

"Sorry. I was with someone."

"And who were you with?"

I could hear her swallow hard on the other end.

"This guy I met at the party. His name is Leo and he's brutally handsome and we may or may not have had sex in the backseat of his car."

"What?!" I exclaimed.

"Don't judge me, Miss I just met Ethan and slept with him the next night."

"Fine. I won't judge, but I called to tell you there was a fire at my apartment building."

"Oh my God! Are you okay?"

"I wasn't home when it started and I'm not sure what damage there is."

"Where the hell are you?"

"I'm at Ethan's house. He insisted I spend the night here since I couldn't get hold of you or Ian."

"Oh. I'm sorry."

"Don't be. I was going to go to a hotel, but he wouldn't let me."

"Hmm," she spoke.

"What's that 'hmm' for?"

"Nothing. Listen, I'm happy you're safe and I'm sorry I didn't answer, but I have to go. Leo and I are heading back to my place."

"Do you know anything about him?"

"As much as you knew about Ethan when you slept with him. Call me tomorrow."

"I will. Love you."

"Love you too, baby doll."

I ended the call and made my way down to the Parlor level where Ethan's office was.

"Are you in here?" I asked as I approached the doorway.

"Yes. How was your bath?" he asked.

"It was good and very relaxing."

"I must say, Aubrey, you look really good in my t-shirt."

I let out a light laugh. "Thanks. Would you mind telling me what color it is?"

I heard the rustling of his pants and soft footsteps as he approached me.

"How about you show me how that app works? The one that tells you the color of your garments."

I pushed the app button and scanned my phone down the t-shirt. It alerted me that the color was black.

"That's really cool," he spoke. "Is it ever wrong?"

"God, I hope not." I laughed.

He let out a chuckle as he lightly took hold of my arm.

"How about a glass of wine before bed?"

"I would like that." I smiled. "If you don't mind, I would like to lead you to the kitchen."

"Be my guest." He let go of my arm.

I pushed the button to the elevator and once we stepped inside, I found the button to the Garden level and pushed it. The doors opened and I stepped out, turning to the right, and making my way to the kitchen.

"See." I grinned. "No need to worry, Mr. Klein. I got this whole blind thing down."

"I'm sorry, Aubrey. It's just—"

"It's just you've never met a blind person before and you can't understand how we do the things we do. I get it. You're not the only person who thinks that. I'm the same as you, Ethan. I can do everything you can do, and I can go to the same places you go. The only difference is I don't have eyesight."

"I know that." He lightly placed his hand on the side of my face.

Taking in a sharp breath, my heart began to rapidly beat.

****

Ethan

While my hand stroked her cheek, my other clenched into a fist. I shouldn't, but I couldn't control myself and I knew she wanted me too. I still had more of her body to explore and the desire inside me was raging out of control. Not to mention my cock, which was getting hard just by looking at her in my t-shirt.

I leaned down and my tongue softly glided over her neck. A light moan escaped her. She didn't push me away as she brought her hands up to my head and her fingers tangled through my hair. I picked her up and her legs wrapped tightly around my waist. Carrying her to the elevator, I took her to her room, sat her on the bed, and pulled my t-shirt over her head. Kneeling down, I took her breasts in my mouth, one at a time, exploring them and gently wrapping my lips around her hardened nipples. Her hands roamed down my body as her fingers gripped the bottom of my shirt, pulling it up and over my head. Standing up, I took down my pants, kicked them to the side, and then pulled the covers back. I was taking this slow with her because I needed to devour every inch of her body. I laid her back so her head rested on the pillow. Her hands planted firmly on my chest. I kept staring at her lips. Parted lips that were begging to be kissed. I was close as I leaned down and could feel the warm air that escaped them. But instead, I slid my tongue down her torso, circling her belly button as her tummy tightened and her back arched with pleasure. Slowly making my way down to her clit, my tongue made tiny teasing circles before sliding up and down her, taking in the wetness that was already there. Placing my hands on her inner thighs, I spread her legs wider and inserted my tongue in her opening. She was so beautiful and her pussy was perfection. As my mouth devoured every inch of her swollen area, my hands reached up and played with her breasts. Her moans increased in loudness and her body tightened around me as she came. I wasn't finished with her yet as I plunged a finger inside and my mouth made its way back up to her.

"I want you on top of me," I whispered in her ear. "I want to watch that beautiful body of yours fuck me until I come."

A smile crossed her lips as I climbed off the bed to get a condom. She grabbed my hand and when I turned and looked at her, she spoke, "I'm on birth control, so you don't need to use a condom."

"Are you sure?"

"I'm positive. I want to feel you and only you."

I climbed into bed and pulled her on top of me, holding her naked body against me. She sat up and took hold of my rock hard cock in her hand, stroking it up and down with a firm grip. Throwing my head back, I gasped at her touch. It was sensual and I was about to explode. Hovering over me, she brushed her clit against the head of my cock before inserting it inside her, slowly pushing down until I was buried deep inside. She moved up and down me like a goddess and circled her hips, causing my arousal to heighten. Her pussy clamped around me as she moved back and forth in a perfect rhythm that sent shivers down my spine and her wetness coated my cock with sheer delight. I fondled her breasts as she rode me, fingering her hard nipples and taking in the glorious sight before me. I'd never seen a more beautiful woman than I was seeing at that moment. Her hair that fell over her shoulders, the upward curve of her mouth that produced an exquisite smile, and her palms that were firmly planted on my chest. Loud moans escaped us both as her movements became rapid. Her clit swelled against my cock and she was about to come.

"Come for me, baby," I panted. "As soon as you come, I will. I'm holding back for you."

I grasped her hips and moved her back and forth against me, intensifying the pleasure for both of us. She howled as I felt the warmth pour from her and my cock exploded while I held her still and strained to make sure I filled her with every last drop I had in me. She collapsed on my chest. Her breasts pressed firmly against me. Wrapping my arms tightly around her back, I held her and we lay there until our heart rates slowed.

She rolled off of me and lay on her side, as did I. Bringing my hand to her cheek, I ran my finger down it and smiled. Even though I knew she couldn't see my smile, I didn't care.

"You were amazing," I spoke.

"So were you." She smiled.

I knew I needed to leave, but I didn't want to just yet, so I lay on my back and pulled her into me, holding her tight.

"Can I ask you something?" I spoke.

"Of course."

"You don't seem upset about your apartment building. I thought maybe you'd be all stressed out or something, but you haven't spoken a single word about it."

"I'm okay, my aunt is okay, and the rest of the tenants are okay. Nobody was hurt and that's all that matters."

"Aren't you worried about your stuff? The damage to your apartment?"

"Not really. Those are all material things and they can easily be replaced and my apartment can be fixed. Everything will work out."

The strength that this woman possessed amazed me. I lay there, staring up at the ceiling as my finger caressed her arm and the demons inside me tried to claw their way out.

"I guess I should go to my room now."

There was silence. No response from her. I looked down and saw she was sound asleep, an angel who was worn out from the activities of the night. I sighed, for I didn't want to wake her. Maybe I'd just close my eyes for a while and when I awoke, she'd have moved and I could quietly leave.

Chapter 14
Aubrey

My eyes opened to the sounds of Ethan mumbling something in his sleep. His legs were restless and I could feel him tossing and turning. I couldn't quite make out what he was saying, but he was definitely having a nightmare.

"Ethan," I softly spoke as I reached over and touched his arm, which was covered in sweat.

He jerked it away from me and I heard the rustling of the sheets as he rolled over on his side. I reached out to touch him and placed my hand on his back. He was soaked and still mumbling. But this time, his mumbles grew louder and then suddenly, they stopped. I lay there for a moment, waiting, wondering if he had awoken from his nightmare.

"Ethan, are you okay?"

I could hear the sharp intake of his breath before he spoke.

"I'm fine, Aubrey. Go back to sleep."

"Are you sure?"

"I said go back to sleep," he spoke in a commanding tone.

Rolling over, I pulled the sheet close to me and closed my eyes. After a few moments, I heard his feet hit the floor, the door open, and before I knew it, he was gone. I tried to go back to sleep, but I couldn't. Whatever that dream he had was about, it rattled him and I got the feeling that it wasn't the first time he had it.

The next morning, I pushed the time app on my phone and it alerted me that it was eight o'clock. I climbed out of bed, put on Ethan's t-shirt, and headed downstairs to see if he was up. When I walked into the kitchen, I called for Ethan but got no response.

"Oh, hello," a female voice from behind spoke.

"Hello."

"May I help you with something?" she asked.

"I was looking for Ethan."

"I'm sorry, but who are you?"

"I'm Aubrey." I held out my hand.

"Nice to meet you, Aubrey. I'm Ingrid, Ethan's housekeeper." She placed her hand in mine. "Did you spend the night?"

"Yes. Upstairs in the guest bedroom. Ethan was kind enough to let me stay since there was a fire in my apartment building last night and everyone was evacuated."

"Oh. I'm sorry to hear that. Did you check in his office?"

"No. I just came down here first."

"Sometimes he goes out for a run in the mornings. Why don't you sit down and I'll make you some coffee?"

"Thank you. That would be nice."

I ran my hand along the edge of the island until I felt the tall chairs that sat in front of it.

"Just in case you're wondering, I'm blind," I spoke as I took a seat.

"Really? I never would have—Okay, I didn't want to ask. I'm sorry."

I softly laughed. "Don't be sorry. I kind of like to get that out of the way."

"Well, you just sit right there and let me make you some breakfast. I'll get the coffee started right now."

I folded my hands as I sat at the island and waited for the coffee to brew. I couldn't stop thinking about last night. Not only the mind-blowing sex we had, but also the nightmare that sent Ethan out of my room.

"So, how do you know Ethan?" Ingrid asked.

"We met at my best friend's art exhibition and then we ran into each other last night at a party. We were out in SoHo when I got the call about my apartment building."

I heard a door open and footsteps walk into the kitchen.

"Ingrid, what are you doing here? Today's your one Sunday off a month."

"I forgot my grocery list yesterday and I just came back to get it when I met Aubrey."

"Good morning, Ethan," I spoke.

"Morning, Aubrey," he spoke with a flat tone.

"Did you have a good run?" Ingrid asked.

"Yeah. It was okay. I need to go shower. I'll be down after."

"Do you want breakfast?" she shouted as I heard his footsteps running up the stairs.

"No. I'll grab some coffee when I come down."

I sat there with a heavy heart that he could treat me like he did after our night together. I was confused and wondered if I had done something wrong.

"Here's your coffee, honey."

"Thank you."

"I make the best Belgian waffles and they're Ethan's favorite. How about I whip up a batch and I bet he'll be down here the minute he smells them."

"It's your day off, Ingrid. I'm fine with just coffee. I'm not very hungry anyway."

She placed her hand on mine. "Listen, honey. Don't let that man get you down. I know he can be rude and angry and just an overall asshole ninety percent of the time, but deep down, he has a heart of gold. You just have to keep chipping away at all the stone around it before you get there."

I couldn't help but laugh.

"Now, how about some of Ingrid's Belgian waffles?"

"Sure." I smiled.

As I was sitting there, my phone rang and alerted me that my Aunt Charlotte was calling.

"Hello," I answered.

"Hello, sweetheart. I just wanted to let you know that I spoke with the fire department and we won't be able to get back into the apartment until tomorrow. I'm going to stay an extra day and fly out in the morning. Where are you staying?"

"With a friend. I'm fine."

"Okay. Well, I'll see you tomorrow. Love you."

"I love you too, Aunt Charlotte."

I sighed as I ended the call.

"Bad news?" Ingrid asked.

"They aren't letting anyone back inside the building until tomorrow."

"No worries. You can stay here another night."

"Thanks, Ingrid, but I think I've stayed long enough, plus Ethan is going to his parents' house today to celebrate Labor Day. After breakfast, I'm just going to grab my clothes and go."

Chapter 15
Ethan

I couldn't shake the fact that I had another nightmare last night, and what made matters worse was that Aubrey was there. Now she'd start asking questions and I wasn't about to discuss anything with her. I was angry. Angry that the nightmares returned and I had no idea why. I took in a deep breath as I ended my shower and got dressed. As I walked down the stairs and headed to the kitchen, the smell of Ingrid's Belgian waffles smacked me in the face. Damn her.

"I told you I wasn't hungry," I spoke as I walked into the kitchen and over to the coffee pot for a cup of coffee.

"I made them for Aubrey. Not you. So go take your coffee and enjoy it."

Rolling my eyes, I leaned up against the counter and sipped my coffee while staring at Aubrey, who was sitting at the island eating breakfast. Damn, those waffles smelled and looked so good.

"Fine, Ingrid. Give me some waffles." I sighed as I sat down next to Aubrey. "As soon as we're done eating, I'll take you back to your apartment."

"Okay," she softly spoke.

I saw Ingrid glance over at her and then back at me.

"Aubrey got a call and they aren't letting anyone back into the apartment building until tomorrow."

"Is that true?" I asked her.

"Yes. My Aunt Charlotte called. Don't worry. You've helped me enough and I appreciate it." She got up from her chair. "I'm going to go get dressed." She headed towards the elevator.

As soon as the doors closed, Ingrid shot me a look and stood there shaking her head.

"What?"

"First of all, you didn't tell me that the girl who made you dinner was blind. And second of all, you're an asshole."

"How am I an asshole?"

"First, it was your attitude towards her when you came back from your run. And, second, you are not going to sit there and tell me that you didn't sleep with her last night. Because I know you and you can't keep your dick in your pants for nothing when a woman is around."

"You know what? I should fire you right now."

"Go ahead and see who else would put up with you and your bullshit every day."

I rolled my eyes. She was right.

"In fact, you're not worthy of my Belgian waffles." She walked over and took the plate away from me.

"Jesus Christ, Ingrid. What the hell is your problem?"

"That poor girl up there is feeling like she's not welcome here because of you and your attitude. She's not like the others, Ethan."

"Don't you think I know that!" I slammed my fist on the counter. "She's different and she's an incredible woman and I like spending time with her, but it scares the hell out of me. I had another nightmare last night."

"Then I suggest you give Dr. Perry a call and work it out. In the meantime, I think you owe Aubrey an apology."

I sighed as I got up from my chair and went up to Aubrey's room. Lightly knocking on the door, she told me to come in.

"I'm ready to go." She sat on the edge of the bed.

"Where do you think you're going?"

"Penelope's, I guess. I tried to call her again, but she didn't answer. She's probably still with that Leo guy."

I sat down on the edge of the bed and took hold of her hand.

"I'm sorry about last night and I don't want to talk about it. I shouldn't have snapped at you the way I did or given you an attitude when I came in this morning. You have done nothing wrong, Aubrey. You're staying here tonight. Okay?"

"Thank you, Ethan, but it's best if I just go."

"You may think it's best, but I don't. So, it's settled; you're staying here tonight."

"You think so?" She grinned.

"I know so and it's no longer up for discussion."

She laid her head on my shoulder. "Thank you again."

"You're welcome." I kissed the top of her head as I closed my eyes.

My fist clenched at what I was about to ask her next. Was I making the right choice? I didn't know. But what I did know was that it felt right.

"Would you like to come spend the day with me at my parents' house?"

"That's nice of you to ask, but it's your family day and I don't want to intrude. You go and have a good time. I'll be fine."

"You won't be intruding, and if I didn't want you there, I wouldn't have asked."

"I don't want to go in the same clothes as last night and I don't have any makeup on. I'm sure I look like a hot mess."

"Actually, you look beautiful." I smiled.

I had an idea. One that I thought she would enjoy.

"Come with me." I grabbed her hand and pulled her up from the bed.

"Where are we going?"

"You'll see. We'll leave now because we have a stop to make first."

"Is Harry outside already?" she asked.

"Harry isn't driving us. I am."

"You're driving the limo?" She grinned.

"No. I'm driving my personal car."

I led her to the garage and opened the door to the Bentley. She climbed in and ran her hand along the leather seat.

"Sometimes I wish that I could drive." She glanced over at me as I pulled out of the garage.

"Not in New York you don't." I chuckled.

I pulled up to the valet parking at Bloomingdales and helped Aubrey out of the car.

"Are you going to tell me where we are?" she asked.

"Why don't you see if you can guess once we get inside?"

She held on to me as we entered through the doors. Once we were inside, she stopped and stood there for a moment, trying to figure out where we were.

"A large department store. We're either at Bloomingdales or at Bergdorf. But I'm going to say Bloomingdales." She grinned.

I stood there shaking my head in disbelief that she knew exactly where we were.

"How did you know?"

"Because we weren't in the car that long and Bloomingdales is closer to your townhouse."

This woman never ceased to amaze me and I found myself at war between feeling comfortable with her and wanting to run as fast as I could.

"So why are we here?"

"I thought you would like to have your makeup done and then we could get you a new outfit to wear to my parents' house."

"Are you serious?" She smiled as she turned her head in my direction.

"Very serious."

"Ethan. I don't—" She lowered her head.

"We're doing this, Aubrey. I want you to be comfortable at my parents' house. Now, the girl at the Chanel counter isn't busy. Is that okay?"

"Chanel is fine."

I took her over to the counter and a young saleswoman named Vanessa asked if she could help us.

"She would like to get her makeup done."

"Do you have an appointment?" she asked as she looked at Aubrey.

"No, she doesn't. We're heading out for the day and she needs her makeup done."

"I'm sorry, sir, but we do makeup by appointment only."

I sighed as I pulled my wallet from my pocket and took out a hundred-dollar bill.

"This should cover the makeup session plus we'll be buying whatever makeup you use. I do believe you work on commission, correct?"

"Yes, sir." She smiled. "Please have a seat—"

"Aubrey. Her name is Aubrey and she is visually impaired."

"Oh. Okay. Do you usually wear makeup?" she asked her.

"Yes. I wear it every day."

"Great. I'll go pick a foundation to match your skin tone and we'll get started."

While Aubrey was getting her makeup done, I pulled my phone out, stepped away, and called my mother.

"Hello."

"Hey, Mom."

"Ethan. You better not be calling to say you're not coming."

"I'm not. I'm calling to let you know that I will be bringing someone with me."

"Oh. Who?"

"Her name is Aubrey."

"Ethan! That's wonderful. I can't wait to meet her. How long have you been dating her?"

"We're not dating, Mom. We're friends. Her apartment building had a fire last night and she will be staying at my place for a couple of days. I thought since she was there, she should come instead of staying home alone."

"Perfect. I can't wait to tell your sister."

"Mom, she's not my girlfriend, so don't go saying that she is. She's just a friend of mine. There's something you need to know about her before we come over."

"What?"

"She's blind."

"Oh dear. Thanks for letting me know."

"We'll see you soon, Mom."

"Bye, darling."

Placing my phone back in my pocket, I walked over to where Aubrey was sitting and smiled as I looked at her made-up face.

"She's all done. What do you think?"

"I think she looks absolutely beautiful." I smiled.

"So you would like to purchase all the products I used?" Vanessa grinned.

"Yes, just put it on my account here."

"Your name?"

"Ethan Klein."

"Thank you, Mr. Klein." She smiled and then turned to Aubrey. "Your boyfriend is a keeper. You better hold on tight to him."

"He's not my boyfriend. He's my pimp." Aubrey smirked as she got up from the stool and lightly grabbed hold of my arm.

I looked at Vanessa, who was standing there with a shocked expression on her face, and gave her a wink.

As we were taking the escalator to the next level where the women's clothing was, I asked Aubrey why she said that.

"Because she shouldn't just assume things like that."

"True. But a pimp? Really?"

"Did you want me to say you were my gay best friend?" She arched her brow.

"I suppose pimp was fine." I chuckled as I stopped at a rack of long dresses.

"You like long dresses, right? I've seen you in a couple of them. Here's a rack of very casual looking ones. Perfect for a barbeque, I think."

She took the fabric of one of the dresses on the rack and felt it between her fingers.

"This feels nice. What does it look like?"

"It's navy blue with small white flowers all over it."

I pulled it from the rack and held it up while she felt the neckline and ran her hands all the way down the dress.

"I'll have to try it on. Do they have a small?"

I looked at the tag on the inside of the dress and smiled.

"This one is a small."

"Lead the way to the fitting room, Mr. Klein." She held on to my arm.

The sales associate opened up a dressing room for her and I took a seat on the chair that was sitting right outside. After a few moments, Aubrey called my name and I stepped inside to see how stunning she looked in that dress.

"How does it look on me?" she asked.

"It's perfect. You look beautiful."

"You're not just saying that, are you?" She smirked.

"No. If I didn't like it, I would tell you. I don't hold back on anything."

"How much is it?"

"Don't you worry about the cost. I'm paying for it."

"No, Ethan. You already paid for my makeup. I can buy myself a dress."

"It's going on my account, Aubrey. End of discussion."

"Is everything okay in here?" the sales associate asked as she walked up.

"Yes. I'll be buying that dress and she will be wearing it out of the store."

"Very good. Just follow me and I'll ring you up and remove the sensor and the tags."

I walked inside the dressing room and grabbed Aubrey's other clothes.

"Do you need shoes?" I asked.

"No. The white sandals I'm wearing are fine."

I led her over to the cash register, picked up a piece of paper and a pen, and wrote a note to the sales associate.

"My friend is blind and I don't want her knowing how much the dress costs. Please do not say the total out loud." I handed the note to her.

She read it and then looked at me with a smile.

"You can just put the dress on my account. The name is Ethan Klein."

"You're all set, Mr. Klein. Thank you for shopping at Bloomindales." She nodded her head.

I had the valet bring the car around and we set out to my parents' house.

Chapter 16
Aubrey

I was very appreciative of Ethan's generosity and he made me feel special. The kind of special that I had never felt before. I was slowly falling for this man and I didn't want to, but he was making it impossible with the sweet things he had done for me. I remembered his comment about never wanting a family and it made me curious as to why he felt that way. Did I dare ask him now? That probably wasn't a good idea since I didn't want to stir up anything before arriving at his parents' house.

"We're here," Ethan announced as the car stopped.

"I'm a little nervous."

"Don't be. My parents are great people and they will welcome you with open arms."

As Ethan helped me out of the car, my phone rang and alerted me that Ian was calling.

"Let me answer this for a second," I spoke.

"Go ahead."

"It's about time you returned my call," I answered.

"Oh sorry. I didn't know you called. My phone got stolen last night at the club and I had to get a new one this morning."

"That's a bummer."

"I know. I was just calling to see if you wanted to hang out today. A bunch of us are getting together in Central Park for a barbeque."

"That sounds great, but I'm spending the day with Ethan. In fact, we just arrived at his parents' house, so I'll call you later."

"Wait. What? You lost me at you were spending the day with Ethan. He called you?"

"Bye, Ian. We'll talk later."

After ending the call, I slipped my phone back inside my purse and lightly took hold of Ian's arm as he guided me up to the house. It was a beautiful, warm and sunny day and perfect for a family get-together.

The minute we stepped inside the door, I heard footsteps coming from all directions.

"You made it!" a cheerful woman's voice spoke.

"It's about time, big brother."

"Good to see you, son."

"Everyone, I would like you to meet my friend, Aubrey Callahan. Aubrey, to the right of you is my sister Lila."

"It's nice to meet you, Lila."

"It's nice to meet you too, Aubrey. Do you mind if I hug you? We're a family of huggers."

I gave her a smile and we lightly hugged.

"Standing in front of you is my mother, Nancy."

"Aubrey, you're gorgeous. Welcome to our home. It's so good to meet you." She hugged me tight.

"Thank you. It's nice to meet you as well."

"And over to your left is my father, Joe."

"Nice to meet you, Aubrey." He hugged me.

"Nice to meet you too."

Their home felt warm and inviting with a lemon scent that filtered in the air.

"Come on. Let's go out on the patio and have some drinks," Nancy spoke.

I placed my hand on Ethan's arm as he led me outside.

"There's a large step out the door," he spoke.

I stepped down and he took me over to the patio table and pulled out a chair for me.

"Thank you." I smiled.

"What can I get you to drink?" he asked.

"Whatever you're having is fine."

"I'm going to have a beer."

"A beer sounds good."

"Really? You drink beer?"

"Yeah. I drink beer." I grinned.

"Two beers coming right up."

When Ethan went off to get a couple of beers, Nancy reached over and grabbed my hand.

"You are the first girl Ethan has brought around since—"

"Mom, we aren't supposed to talk about that," Lila chimed in.

"Aren't supposed to talk about what?" Ethan asked as he set the beer bottle down in front of me.

"The accident I had the other day with my car," Lila spoke nervously.

"You were in an accident?" Ethan asked.

"Not really. I just backed up too far and hit the brick on the garage. I feel really stupid about it and I didn't want it talked about."

"You should. How the hell did you do that?" Ethan chuckled.

"Like I said, we aren't supposed to talk about it, so drop it."

I let out a light laugh.

"By the way, where's Kenny?" Ethan asked.

"He's on his way. Why? Do you miss him or something?"

"No. It's just the two of you are like Siamese twins. It's weird just seeing half of you."

"Shut up, Ethan." Lila laughed.

As I sat there and listened to the banter between him and his sister, my mind kept wandering to what his mom said about me being the first girl he had brought around "since." But what really piqued my curiosity was that Lila said they weren't supposed to talk about it. How long had it been? Two years? Three years? Was she the reason he said he never wanted a family? The more time I spent with him, the more questions I had. He was a very closed off man, that much I already knew, and I had a feeling that he wasn't going to tell me anything about his past.

"Do you work, Aubrey?" Nancy asked.

"Yes. I teach English Literature over at Roosevelt High."

"Wow. How wonderful. How long have you been teaching?"

"This is my second year."

"That's amazing. Good for you, honey." She patted my hand. "If you'll excuse me, I'm going to get some things prepped for dinner."

"May I help with something?"

"No, honey. You're a guest in our home. You just sit there and relax. There's not much to do."

The one thing people didn't understand about the visually impaired was that we were capable of doing everything that those with sight could. I often wondered that when people told me just to sit and relax, if it was their way of not trusting me. That was the biggest obstacle in my life since I lost my sight. People believed that because I couldn't see, I couldn't do. It was their non-belief that fueled me to do everything I could and more to the best of my ability all these years.

"Ethan, come in the house with me. I got a new set of golf clubs the other day that I want to show you."

"Sure, Dad. I'll be back, Aubrey," he spoke to me.

"Okay. I'll be here." I smiled.

"So, how did you and my brother meet?" Lila asked.

"We met at an art gallery where my best friend was having her first art exhibition. He asked me out and I told him no. Then he asked my friend, the artist, for my number. She refused to give it to him but told him where I go on Saturday mornings."

"Where do you go?"

"I go to Shakespeare Garden in Central Park to read for a couple of hours. I was sitting there the next morning and he claimed he was taking a stroll."

Lila let out a loud laugh. "My brother? Taking a stroll? You didn't buy that, did you?"

"No." I smiled. "I invited him over for dinner and we had a nice night. Then last night, we ran into each other again at his friend's party."

"And now you're here meeting the family," she spoke. "Interesting."

"Interesting?"

"You're the first girl we've met in nine years. You must be pretty special to him."

"I don't think so. We haven't known each other that long. He didn't want me to sit home alone all day since I'm staying with him until I can get back into my apartment. Are the two of you close?" I asked.

"We used to be. But he doesn't come around much and hasn't for years. Ever since Sophia, he's changed and not in a good way."

"Sophia?"

"Shit. Listen, you have to promise not to tell him that I told you. We aren't allowed to talk about it and if he catches us, he'll be so pissed off and who knows what he'll do."

"I promise I won't. You can trust me."

"Sophia was his girlfriend who passed away in a terrible accident. I've said too much already. Let's go inside and see if my mom needs any help."

"Sure. Okay." I got up from my chair.

Finally, I knew a little more about him. A tragedy that struck his heart and a hurt so deep that it still affected him all these years later.

Chapter 17
Ethan

My parents and Lila liked Aubrey. In fact, I was pretty sure they fell in love with her the moment they met her. I knew they would and I knew this could cause a potential problem for me. The problem was that my mother wouldn't leave me alone about her. Lila and Aubrey went outside while my mother asked me to stay back and help her for a moment. But I knew damn well she didn't need help with anything.

"Aubrey is a very nice girl, Ethan."

"Yes. She is."

"It's incredible to me that she's a teacher. She's a very strong woman."

"Yes. She is."

"She's very sweet."

"Yes. She is," I spoke because I knew exactly where this was going.

"So does this mean that the two of you will be spending a lot of time together?" she asked innocently.

"No. It does not. I already told you that Aubrey and I are friends and nothing more."

"But you brought her home to us."

"Because I didn't want her staying at my house all alone. That's the only reason, Mother."

I walked over and clasped her shoulders.

"We're just friends. Please don't read any more into it."

"Ethan—"

"Friends, Mother. Now drop it," I spoke as I walked out to the patio.

I knew this would happen if I brought her here because my mother couldn't understand that I wasn't interested in any type of relationship, so I shut her down quickly. When I walked outside, I took a seat next to Aubrey. Not too long after, Kenny showed up and dinner was served. After we ate, Kenny, my dad, and I all shot some golf balls and bullshitted about life. Every time I glanced over at Aubrey, which I found myself doing more than I should have, she was laughing, smiling, and enjoying the conversations she was having with my mother and sister. A feeling stirred inside me that was getting harder to control. It was getting late, so I asked Aubrey if she was ready to go. After saying goodbye to my family, we climbed in the car and headed back to the city.

"I didn't know your dad was a chief technology officer for a company on Wall Street," she spoke.

"He was until he had a heart attack a few years ago and decided to retire. He said the stress and the demands of the job just weren't worth it anymore."

"You must get your technology smarts from him." She smiled.

"I guess so." I smiled back.

"How did you get to owning your own company at such a young age?"

"I'd always been a tech geek, so to speak. I always looked at technology and thought if I could make whatever it was I was interested in better, I would. I started web designing when I was fifteen, coding when I was sixteen, created and sold two video games to Nintendo and an app worth a lot of money to Apple by the time I was twenty. I did what any twenty-year-old would do after scoring his first few million and traveled for a while. When I was twenty-one, I started Klein Technology. I rented a space, hired some staff, and here I am nine years later."

"You should be very proud of yourself."

"Thanks, Aubrey." I glanced over at her. "Did you have a good time today?"

"I did. Your family is wonderful. I think it's great that your sister is an editorial assistant over at *Elle* magazine. Since she works in the city, do you see her a lot?"

"Not really. Occasionally, I'll run into her at a restaurant. Sometimes, if she's over by my office, she'll drop in and say hi."

Finally, we arrived back at my town house. After parking the car, I got out and opened the door for Aubrey, took her hand and helped her out. Stepping into the house, I placed my hand on the small of Aubrey's back.

"Would you like a glass of wine?" I asked.

"Maybe just a half of glass."

I told her to stay put while I went into the living room and walked over to the bar, where I grabbed a bottle of wine and two wine glasses and brought them to the kitchen. I had sex on my mind all day long and thoughts of her underneath me aroused me on more than one occasion. I found myself needing her and wanting her more than I should have. After pouring a half of glass, I walked up behind her, took her hand, and placed the wine in it.

"Here you go," I whispered in her ear as I moved her hair to one side.

"Thank you."

"You're welcome." My lips lightly pressed into her neck.

She slightly tilted her head to the side to allow me full access. That was her way of telling me not to stop. Taking the glass out of her hand, I set it down on the counter. My cock was getting harder by the second as my fingers took hold of her straps and pushed them off her shoulders, letting her dress fall to the floor. Unhooking her bra, I tossed it to side and wrapped my arm around her breasts, feeling her hardened nipples pressed against my skin while my tongue traced circles around her soft neck. She gasped as I placed my other hand firmly against her stomach and my fingers traveled down the front of her panties, not stopping until they reached her wet opening and dipped inside her. I felt her body tremble as I firmly held her against me, pressing my hard and throbbing cock against her. Several moans escaped her lips while my fingers explored her and my tongue devoured every inch of her neck.

"Do you want to come?" I whispered in her ear.

"Yes. God, yes."

I tightened my grip around her as my fingers moved in circles, hitting the right spot that sent her body into an explosion. Her cries of ecstasy heightened as her body stiffened in my arms and she orgasmed. I smiled as I turned her around and explored her breasts with my mouth, making my way down her torso before getting on my knees and tasting the sweetness that emerged from her.

"I need you right now," I softly spoke. "I need to be inside you." I lifted her up and placed her on the granite countertop.

Wrapping her legs around my waist, I thrust inside her, hard and deep until my cock was enshrouded by her warmth. Placing my hands on each side of her face, I tilted her head slightly up so our eyes met. I wished she could see how unraveled I became when I was fucking her. To see the pleasure she gave me each time I thrust in and out of her. The pressure was building and I was getting ready to explode. She placed her hands on the counter and leaned back as I grabbed her hips and held her steady, pounding into her at a rapid pace. Both of us moaned in excitement as our bodies synced together and we came at the same time. I halted and strained to pour every last drop inside her.

I picked her up, her legs still tight around my waist. She wrapped her arms around my neck and laid her head on my shoulder in exhaustion while I carried her to the elevator and took her up to her room. Laying her down on the bed, I pulled out of her and stroked her hair as I rolled on my side.

"I have a confession to make," she spoke as she turned her head towards me.

"What's that?"

"You are the only man that I've slept with who has given me orgasms during sex."

Hearing her say that made me smile, but also an unbearable rage of jealousy crept inside me knowing that she'd slept with other men. I knew I had no right to feel that way, but I did and it bothered me.

"That's a good thing, right?"

"Of course it is." She laughed as she brought her hand to my cheek. "You're an amazing man."

"Not that amazing, Aubrey."

"To me you are." She smiled.

Things were getting heated between us and I was too frightened to continue this type of conversation.

"I should go to my room now and let you get some sleep." I sat up and placed my feet on the floor.

"Please don't go. Just stay with me tonight. Please, Ethan." She placed the palm of her hand firmly against my back.

I sat there, clenching my fist while I closed my eyes and took in a deep breath. I wanted to stay with her and feel her body wrapped around mine all night. But what if I had another nightmare?

"I know something is going on with you and I know you had a nightmare last night. I don't need to know what it was about and you don't have to tell me. I just want you to stay."

"You don't understand, Aubrey. I don't do this. I don't stay. I fuck and I get out. It's best that way for both you and me."

"So is that what we just did? We fucked? Because I know it was more than that. I felt it from you. In the way you touched me."

"I do that to all the women I fuck. I'm sorry if you read anything more into it. It's just sex, Aubrey. I'm a man and I have needs. You're a woman and you can fulfill those needs. I can't, nor will I ever give you anything more. I don't have it in me." I stood up and walked towards the door.

"My Aunt Charlotte was right about you," she spoke. "And so was Ian when he told me that people call you 'The Iceman.' Now I understand why. But if you want my opinion, I think you're hiding. You're carefully guarding yourself because of Sophia."

I whipped my head around and spoke in anger. "How the hell do you know about Sophia?"

"Your sister accidentally mentioned her. She didn't mean to; it just slipped out. What happened to her, Ethan?"

"I don't discuss that and you are to never speak of her again. Do you understand me?" I spoke in a commanding and angered voice.

"No, actually, I don't understand and I'm not going to lie to you and say I do. We all lose the people we love, but life does and still has to go on."

"Enough!" I shouted. "This discussion is over." I walked out the door.

Chapter 18
Aubrey

I lay there, naked and exposed on the bed as he just walked out the door, leaving my heart broken. A perfect day turned bad because he was too afraid to get close to me. Getting up from the bed, I dressed myself in the clothes that I wore to the party the other night. I needed my phone, but it was down in the kitchen where my purse was. Leaving was the best choice for both of us and I wanted to get out of there as fast as I could. If I took the elevator, he'd hear me, so I took the stairs, remembering that I was on the third floor. I counted the floors as I made my way down each set of staircases until I was on the garden level where the kitchen was. Feeling my way around, I placed my hands on the island where Ethan and I had just made love. I remembered setting my purse down on the table while I was waiting for him to pour me my glass of wine. Making my way to the table, I found it and placed it over my shoulder, and as I was making my way to the door, I heard Ethan's voice behind me.

"Where are you going?"

"I'm going to stay with Penelope for the night."

"Why?" he abruptly asked.

"Because I think after our last conversation, it's for the best."

"Why do you think it's for the best? Because I told you it was just sex and nothing more to me? Seriously, Aubrey? We've known each other for what? A week and a half? Or is it because I won't talk to you about something that's extremely personal to me?"

"I'm done talking about this, Ethan, and you're right, we've only known each other for a very short time and I'm sorry that I let myself believe that maybe, just maybe, I meant a little something more to you than just a fuck buddy."

Silence filled the space between us. Having this conversation with him was slowly tearing me apart and I needed to leave because I refused to break down in front of him. Maybe the other women he had similar conversations with did just that, but I wouldn't give him the satisfaction of knowing that he broke me. The makeup session, the dress, the donuts and coffee, taking me to meet his parents—all of that made me feel like he saw me as something more. But I was wrong and I would tuck my tail between my legs and quietly leave.

"I'm sorry, Aubrey."

"I am too, Ethan."

"At least let me drive you to Penelope's."

"No. I can get there on my own. I don't need any more of your help."

"Then at least let me walk you out and hail you a cab."

"I can get my own cab."

I stepped into the elevator and took it up to the Parlor level and walked out the front door. Pulling my cane from my purse, I tapped each step in front of me as I held on to the railing and made my way to the sidewalk. Standing on the curb, I pulled out my phone and called for a cab.

"Sure thing, Aubrey. Actually, Jessie is over that way. He should be there in about five minutes."

"Thanks, Glenn. I'll be waiting."

For me, in my current situation, five minutes seemed like an eternity. I wondered if Ethan was watching me from his window. While I waited for the cab, I dialed Penelope.

"Hello," she sleepily answered.

"Hey. Did I wake you?"

"Umm. Maybe. What's wrong?"

"Can I stay with you tonight?"

"I thought you were staying at Ethan's."

I tried so hard to hold back the tears, but I couldn't do it anymore as I started to stutter into the phone.

"Things didn't work out."

"Oh, Aubrey. What did he do to you? I'm on my way."

"No. A cab will be here in a few minutes. I already called for one."

"Of course you can stay here. I'll see you soon. I wish you would have called me first. I would have come over there and kicked his pompous no good rich ass."

"I think the cab just pulled up. I'll see you soon."

Opening the door, I climbed inside.

"Hey, Aubrey."

"Hi, Jessie."

"You okay, hon?"

"Not really. 425 East 66th Street, please."

As I sat in the back of the cab, the tears streamed down my face. I was a fool to think that he could even remotely feel something for me, and I was also a fool for believing that I could probably fix him. His words felt like a dagger through my heart and even now, I could still feel it inside me.

"We're here, Aubrey," Jessie spoke.

"Thank you. Just put it on my card. It's on file."

"I know, hon. Feel better, okay?"

"I'll try."

As soon as I climbed out of the cab, I heard Penelope's voice.

"Come here." She wrapped her arm around me as we walked into her building. "What happened?"

"We made love and I asked him to stay with me and he wouldn't. I practically begged him. I'm such a loser."

"No you're not." She opened the door to her apartment and I stepped inside.

"He told me that it was nothing more than sex and that all he does is fuck and leave. I made the mistake of telling him that I felt it was more than that by the way he touched me and he said that's how he does it to all the women he sleeps with. He basically told me that I was nothing special."

"Aw, sweetie." She hugged me tight and led me to the couch. "I warned you about him and now do you understand why?"

"Yes, and I was so stupid to let my guard down. I thought he was different. Do you know what he did for me today?"

"What?"

"He took me to Bloomingdales and I had my makeup done and then he bought me a dress to wear to his parents' house. Who just does that for someone they don't care about?"

"Unfortunately, a lot of loser men with big egos. He wanted something in return for his kindness and you gave it to him."

"His sister told me that his ex-girlfriend, Sophia, died in a tragic accident nine years ago, and ever since then, he hasn't been the same. They barely see him anymore."

"Did she say how she died?"

"No, and they aren't allowed to talk about it. In fact, she told me not to tell him that she told me, but I sort of did." I bit down on my bottom lip.

"Oh no. What did you say to him?"

"I just told him that I thought he was guarding himself because of her."

"And what did he say?"

"He instantly became angry and told me never to speak of her again."

"Wow. So apparently, Sophia is the reason he is the way he is."

"I guess so."

"Then you have to stay away from him, Aubrey. He's not the type of man you need to become involved with. Look, you've only known him for a week or two and he's already said some pretty bad things to you. Those are what are called 'red flags' and believe me, they're flying high for you right now."

"I can't forget him and the time we spent together."

"Let me ask you this. Did he kiss you on the lips yet?"

"No."

"There you go. Drop him like a hot potato. He's toxic, Aubrey, and you don't need that in your life. You'll meet someone without all the baggage who will love you because he can't help but to love you. A man like Ethan Klein isn't capable of love, especially if he's damaged from a past relationship. If it's been nine years like you said, and he still isn't over it, then he never will be."

"Maybe you're right."

"I know I am. Now come on; you can sleep with me in my bed."

"Why were you sleeping earlier? You never go to bed that early."

"I wasn't exactly sleeping."

"Oh God. Was he over?"

"Yeah. After you called, I kicked him out."

"You didn't have to do that. I could have just gone somewhere else."

"Don't be silly. You're my best friend and you come before any guy."

"If you don't mind, I think I'll sleep on the couch." I smirked.

"I just want you to know that I'm rolling my eyes at you. I'll go get you a pillow, blanket, and a nightshirt to wear."

"Thanks. I owe you big time." I reached over and gave her a hug.

"No you don't. Just being my best friend is enough. Promise me no more tears over that douchebag."

"I promise."

Chapter 19
Ethan

I drank myself into oblivion after Aubrey decided to leave and passed out on the couch. My sister had no right to bring up Sophia, and now, Aubrey knew a piece of my past I wanted to keep secret. She said she didn't need to know about her, but I knew damn well her curiosity at some point would get the best of her and she'd start asking questions. I hurt her feelings by what I said and it bothered me. Another reason why I could no longer continue to see her. I was getting too close and everything I had fought to keep buried down inside me was starting to emerge.

I opened my eyes as the sun beat through the windows of the living room, blinding me and making the pounding headache I had intensify. I rolled off the couch and stumbled up the stairs to my bedroom. I reeked of alcohol and it was making me sick. Stumbling into the bathroom, I turned on the shower, stripped out of my clothes, and stood under the warm water, placing my hands on the tiled wall for support. I hadn't been this hungover in years. But that hadn't been what I was thinking about as I kicked back several glasses of scotch. I drank to stop thinking about her and to stop thinking about the pained look on her face after our conversation.

The day had come and gone. I attended a few parties my friends were throwing in honor of Labor Day and then strolled in around midnight. I thought that by staying out all day it would help to get my mind off of Aubrey. But it didn't. Even the numerous women hanging all over me and trying to get me to fuck them didn't take my mind off of her.

****

I awoke feeling like I had been hit by a truck. Another night, another nightmare, and a bad mood took hold of me. I stumbled out of bed, showered, dressed, and headed downstairs to the kitchen.

"Good morning, Ethan." Ingrid smiled as she poured me a cup of fresh coffee.

"Morning," I mumbled.

"Uh-oh," she spoke.

She always knew by the look on my face what type of mood I was in.

"Don't ask me any questions. Not today, Ingrid. I'm in no mood."

"I can tell. So I won't ask."

"Pour this coffee in my travel mug. I need to get to the office."

"What about breakfast?"

"I don't want any breakfast." I scowled.

After taking my travel mug from Ingrid, I grabbed my briefcase and headed towards the door.

"Have a good day, Ethan!" she shouted sarcastically.

"It won't be!" I snapped.

Climbing into the limo, I slammed the door shut. Harry turned around and looked at me.

"I suppose it's not a good morning."

"Just drive." I pulled out my phone.

I heard him sigh as he pulled away from the curb and drove me to the office.

"Holly!" I shouted as I passed her desk. "In my office, now!"

She followed me inside and shut the door.

"Good morning, sir."

I rolled my eyes and sighed as I turned around and looked at her.

"Actually, it's not a good morning and I don't want you to ever assume it is. Understand?"

"Yes, sir." She gulped as she took a seat across from my desk.

"I want the last six months of financial reports on my desk in an hour. Also, I want you to get the product development team up here for a meeting at noon."

"Yes, Mr. Klein. Anything else?"

"Go to the bakery down the street and get me one of their lemon poppy seed muffins."

"I'm on it, sir. There's something I need to discuss with you."

"Are you quitting?" I arched my brow.

"No. I'm pregnant. I just thought you should know."

"Pregnant? Are you serious? Is that going to prevent you from doing your job here at Klein Technology?"

"No. It won't affect it at all."

"I hope not. Because if it does, I'll have to fire you and find someone who I can trust won't be getting pregnant any time soon."

"I understand. You don't have to worry."

"Good. Now get out of here and get my muffin and reports."

She nodded her head as she got up from her chair and timidly walked out of my office. Fuck. Why the hell did she have to go and get pregnant? It was in my best interest to start looking for another assistant ASAP.

Pulling out my phone, I brought up Dr. Perry's number. Maybe it was time I gave her a call to try and get to the bottom of these damn nightmares. I hated the thought of sitting in her office again like I did all those years ago.

"Dr. Perry's office. How can I help you?"

"It's Ethan Klein and I need to see Dr. Perry."

"When were you looking to meet with her?" she asked.

"Today, if possible."

"She's completely booked for the rest of the week, but I can squeeze you in next week."

"Next week isn't good. I need to see her as soon as possible."

"I can put you on the cancellation list and give you a call if someone cancels."

I let out a long, hard sigh.

"Fine."

I ended the call and leaned back in my chair. As I was pondering the idea of taking a vacation, Holly walked in with my muffin.

"Here you go, sir. I'll go pull up those reports now and I've already scheduled your meeting with the product development team."

"Good. You may leave."

As I was eating my muffin and drinking my coffee, my phone rang.

"Ethan Klein."

"Mr. Klein, it's Amanda from Dr. Perry's office. We just had a cancellation for three o'clock. Shall I put you in?"

"Yes. Three o'clock will be fine."

"We'll see you then."

Noon had approached and I headed to the conference room to meet with my product development team.

"Good, you're all here." I took a seat at the head of the table.

"Why the urgent meeting, Ethan?" Rob asked.

"Did you know that there are over four hundred and forty thousand people in New York alone that are visually impaired?"

"Umm. No. I didn't know that," Rob spoke.

"And over two hundred and eight million worldwide."

"Interesting," Terrence spoke as he stroked his chin. "So what does that have to do with Klein Technology?"

"I want us to develop an app, and not just any ordinary app. This app we design will have the ability to scan an entire indoor area and tell the person the layout of the space, guiding them in the direction they need to go and alerting them of objects that are in the way of their path."

"Apple already has something like that."

"But it's not suitable for the visually impaired person. It's not voice over compatible. This app would be, and it would also store previous routes, which could be very useful in hotels, malls, and other large buildings."

"I don't know, Ethan," Rob spoke.

"You don't know?" I glared at him. "You will make it work. I've already started the coding." I threw the paper in my hand down on the table. "Look it over and go from there. This can be done. I know it can. Think of how much Apple would pay for something like this. They can't do it, but we can. And as a little incentive to get your asses in gear on this, once it's complete, I will throw in a ten-thousand-dollar bonus to each of you for your hard work."

"Are you serious?" Terrence asked in shock.

"Dead serious. Now get to work. I want an update in three days. If you have to work all night on this, do it. I want this done quickly."

"May I ask why this is so important to you?" Rob asked.

"It's just something that I think visually impaired people need to make their lives a little easier."

Rob laughed. "Since when do you care about blind people, Ethan?"

I shot him a look from across the room.

"I have a friend who is completely blind. That concludes this meeting. Now get out of here and get to work." I looked at my watch. "I have to leave for an appointment."

Chapter 20
Aubrey

The school day came to an end and I was exhausted. Ian walked into the room just as I was packing my bag.

"Hello, princess. Are you ready to leave?"

"Yeah." I sighed.

"What's wrong?"

"Nothing."

He walked over and placed his finger on my chin, slightly lifting my head.

"Are you still thinking about him?"

"Maybe. I can't help it, Ian. He swept me off my feet."

"Listen, sweetheart. He's no good for you. You don't need a man like that, especially with so much baggage in your life. You're too good for him. You're a kind and sweet girl who deserves a man that will love you forever. Someone you can trust."

"You sound like Penelope."

He laughed. "It's the truth. Any reasonable person can see that."

"So you're saying I'm not reasonable?"

He kissed my forehead and took my bag from me. "No. I'm saying you're a woman with a broken heart right now, and when your heart heals, you'll be more reasonable."

I let out a sigh. "You know I hate you, right?"

"Of course you do. Now let's go home. I have a date tonight."

"A date? With whom, may I ask?"

"His name is Rigby."

"He sounds like a dog." I smirked.

"Oh, my dear Aubrey. He's far from a dog. He's tall, tanned, dreamy chocolate eyes, and he has the whitest teeth I've ever seen."

"And when did you meet this Mr. Rigby?"

"Last night when I was at Starbucks getting an iced coffee. He was standing in front of me and when he went to get his wallet, he realized he left it at home. So, being the kind gentleman I am, I paid for his drink."

"Smooth." I grinned.

"He only lived a block away, so I followed him home. He paid me back and we exchanged phone numbers."

"And why am I just hearing about this now? Why didn't you tell me this morning?"

"Because I was waiting to see if he'd make the first move, and he did. He texted me this afternoon and asked me if I wanted to go to dinner."

"That's great, Ian. I want to hear all about it tomorrow morning."

After climbing out of his car, I walked into my building and up to my apartment. I was one of the lucky ones who didn't have any smoke damage. Walking into the kitchen, I opened the refrigerator and took out the container of last night's leftovers of chicken and pasta from the Italian restaurant down the street. Just as I popped it into the microwave, my Aunt Charlotte knocked on the door.

"Honey, it's me. I heard you come home."

Walking over to the door, I opened it and let her in.

"Hi, Aunt Charlotte."

"Hello, honey. Is this a bad time?"

"No. Come on in."

I felt bad because I never told her that Ethan was the one I stayed with. In fact, I didn't tell her anything at all about him. As far as she knew, we had dinner that one night and everything went well. I didn't want to hear her tell me how she was right and I should have listened to her.

"The fire started in Mr. Johnson's apartment. Apparently, he was making something on the stove and forgot about it. Stupid man. He could have easily burned this place down."

"But he didn't and everyone is okay. So we need to thank God for that. Would you like some chicken and pasta?" I asked as I took the container out of the microwave.

"No thank you. I'm having dinner with Mr. Morris tonight."

"Mr. Morris down in 1C?"

"Yes. That Mr. Morris."

"He's been asking you out for a year. Why did you decide to go out with him now?"

"I think it's time I start to explore what's out there and we always have nice conversations. He's a good man. By the way, speaking of men, have you heard from Ethan?"

"Umm. Yeah. We went out and there really isn't a connection there, so I probably won't be seeing him again."

"Oh. Well, it's for the best anyway. I already told you how I felt about him. You deserve much better. I need to get going, sweetheart. I have to get ready for my date," she spoke with excitement.

"Have a good time." I smiled.

After she left, I sat there and ate my dinner while I thought about Ethan. I didn't want to think about him, trust me. But, somehow and someway, he left his mark on me and he wasn't so easy to forget. But I had no choice; I needed to forget about him and the short time we spent together. As much as I didn't want to allow myself to fall for him, I did. I did everything wrong and everything that was out of character for me. I had sex way too fast, I fell too hard too quickly, and in the end, I let him break my heart. Stupid. Stupid. Stupid on my part.

Now Penelope was seeing Leo, Ian was going on a date, and my Aunt Charlotte was spending time with the guy down in 1C. I felt alone at the moment and felt sorry for myself, thinking that I might never find the right man to build a future with and have a family of my own.

Chapter 21
Ethan

"It's been a long time, Ethan. Please have a seat," Dr. Perry spoke. "What brings you back to my office?"

I took a seat in the chestnut-colored, oversized leather chair and placed my arms on the armrest, bringing my ankle up to my leg.

"The nightmares are back."

"When did they return?" she asked as she adjusted her glasses.

"About a week ago."

"Hmm. Did anything in your life change? Possibly something you did or saw that triggered the memory?"

"No." I looked down.

"I get the feeling, Ethan, that you aren't telling me everything."

Letting out a long sigh, I got up from the chair and paced around the room with my hands in my pants pockets. I used to do that during my sessions because it felt more comfortable to me. Dr. Perry understood that and didn't seem to mind.

"They started after I met someone."

"Okay." She nodded. "Why don't you tell me about her?"

"Her name is Aubrey. She's an English Literature teacher over at Roosevelt High School."

"How old is she?"

"Twenty-five."

"Go on," she slowly spoke.

"I don't know what else to say except that she's blind."

Dr. Perry cocked her head when I said that and removed the glasses from her face.

"She's blind?"

"Yes. But I didn't know she was blind when I first met her. I asked her out first and she told me no. Then she proceeded to tell me about her loss of vision."

"Was she born blind?"

"No. She was in a car accident when she was eight years old that also killed both of her parents."

"That poor girl. Did you sleep with her?"

"Yes. A few times."

"And the nightmares returned after you slept with her?"

"Yes. That first night."

I had enough pacing around, so I sat back down.

"Do you have feelings for her?"

"I don't know."

"Ethan, you know how this works. You have to be totally open and honest with me."

"I sleep with a lot of women and I have rules."

"Yes, I know of your rules." She nodded. "Those were rules you put in place to protect yourself since Sophia."

I swallowed hard. "I like being with her and I think about her all the time. She's different from anyone I've known."

"Different how?"

"I don't know. I can't explain it."

"Try."

"She's beautiful and smart. At first, I was incredibly attracted to her physically. I knew the moment I laid eyes on her, I had to have her."

"Sexually?" she asked.

"After she declined my invitation to go out for a drink, I asked her friend about her and she told me that on Saturday mornings, she goes to Shakespeare Garden to read. So, that next morning, I went there."

"And what happened?"

"I was just going to keep my distance at first, like some kind of fucking stalker. But then, she knew I was there, which really caught me off guard."

"How did she know?"

"She could smell my cologne and she just knew it was me. Her senses are incredible. So, we talked and I asked her out and she invited me over for dinner that night."

"She cooked for you?"

"Yes and it was very good. After dinner, we had sex and the first nightmare came that night."

"While you were with her?"

"No. After we had sex, I left and went home. I didn't call or see her that whole week."

"Why?" she asked.

"Because I got what I wanted and I was done with her."

"I don't believe that. I think you started to have some sort of feelings for her and you ran."

I looked down and shifted in my chair.

"Maybe I did. Things were happening to me that haven't in a very long time. Then, a week later, I ran into her at a friend's birthday party. I didn't know she would be there."

"What happened when you saw her again? I would assume she wanted some sort of explanation as to why you never called her after that night."

"I told her I was busy, but she wasn't buying it. She told me that she didn't expect me to call."

"And how did that make you feel when she said that?"

"A little shocked, to be honest. Anyway, we ended up going out that night and while we were taking a walk in SoHo, she got a call that there was a fire in her apartment building and they weren't allowing any of the tenants to stay there that night."

"What happened then?"

"She tried to call a couple of her friends, but they didn't answer, so I invited her to stay at my place for the night."

"Really?" she spoke as she arched her brow. "And how did that go?"

"Fine. Except I was lying with her and fell asleep and had another nightmare. I left the room and didn't speak of it. The next day, I invited her to my parents' house and we had a good time. My sister told her about Sophia, which really pissed me off."

"Why did that piss you off?"

"Because she had no right. What happened in my past is nobody's business. When we got back to my place, we had sex again. She asked me to stay with her and I couldn't. So we got into an argument, she brought up Sophia, I said some things, and she left."

"How did her leaving make you feel?"

"Angry. Very angry. I told her she was no different from any other woman I had slept with and that I was sorry if she got the wrong impression."

"But she is different from the other women and you know that. Your fear, Ethan, is what stirred up the nightmares again. You're afraid because for so long, you could control your feelings and emotions. Now Aubrey walked into your life and you feel that control slipping away and you don't know how to handle it."

I sat there with my fist to my chin, listening to what Dr. Perry was saying.

"Time's up, Ethan." She got up from her chair. "I want to see you again in a couple of days."

"I have back to back meetings for the next week. Is there any way you can come to my house for a private session? I will pay you triple your normal fee."

"I suppose I could." She walked over to her desk and looked at her calendar. "How about Thursday at eight o'clock? My last appointment is at six."

"That's fine. I'll make sure I'm home."

"In the meantime, you need to do some self-reflecting. Maybe give Aubrey a friendly call and see where she stands. I can tell you're not at peace with what happened and I think calling her is a step in the right direction."

"We'll see. I'm sure she hates me."

"She may or may not. There's only one way to find out."

I walked out of the building and hailed a cab back to the office.

Chapter 22
Aubrey

After getting home from another day of school, I set my things down, changed my clothes, and sat at my computer to begin listening to the essays I had my students email me. After listening to about ten of them, I was getting hungry, so I decided to take a break and walk to my favorite Thai restaurant a few blocks away.

"Hello, Miss Aubrey. How are you this evening?"

"I'm good, Kai." I gently smiled.

He took hold of my arm. "Come on, I'll take you to your table and Gwen will be right over. Can I get you something to drink?"

"Just water will be fine. Thank you."

"Hey, Aubrey. It's good to see you. Are you ready to order?" Gwen asked in a cheerful voice.

"Hi, Gwen. I'm going have the Pad Thai tonight with chicken."

"Medium spice okay?"

"That's fine."

"Great. I'll put that order in for you. Would you like a spring roll to go with that?"

"Sure. A spring roll sounds good."

As I sat there and waited for my food, I thought about the conversation Ian and I had this morning about his date with Rigby. Things went so well that they were seeing each other again tonight. Rigby Jones was a financial officer over at Chase Bank and he hadn't been in a relationship in over a year, just like Ian. When he was telling me about his date this morning, his voice was excited and I could tell he was happy. I got the impression that he was already head over heels for him, which I believed could happen after one date. After all, it did happen to me.

After finishing my dinner, Gwen boxed up the leftovers for me.

"Have a great night, Aubrey. Hopefully, we'll see you soon."

"Thanks, Gwen. Have a good night."

Opening the door and stepping out, I walked down the street, tapping my cane in front of me. As I turned the corner, I abruptly stopped when my cane hit something or someone standing in front of me. That scent. It was him.

"Aubrey."

"Ethan."

"How are you?"

"I'm fine. Thank you for asking."

"Did you just come from dinner?" he asked.

"Yes," I replied as I held up my container. "What are you doing over here?"

"I had a dinner meeting, and as I was walking out of the restaurant, I saw you."

"So you decided to stop in front of me?"

"I guess so."

"I need to get home, Ethan. I have a lot of essays to grade."

"Please wait. There's something I need to say first."

"What?"

"I'm sorry for what happened and what I said the other night. I just wanted you to know that. I didn't mean to hurt you."

I stood there, taking in his scent and trying to hold my composure. He sounded sincere and, even though he broke my heart, I accepted his apology.

"I accept your apology."

"Thank you. It means a lot to me."

"Now, if you'll excuse me, I have to get home."

"Please let Harry drive you. He's just around the corner."

"No. I can walk. Enjoy the rest of your evening, Mr. Klein," I spoke as I moved to the side and walked away.

It was nice that Ethan apologized, but it made me wonder if he would have called and said he was sorry if he hadn't run into me. A part of me believed he would because if he didn't stop me, I never would have known he was in the same area. He could have just kept going, but he didn't. I appreciated his apology and it took away some of the bitterness I had towards him for saying what he did, but it didn't change the fact that I needed to move on and forget about him, which I felt I could do now. It was going to be tough, but I'd overcome tougher situations in my life and I survived.

As I stuck the key into the lock of my apartment door, I heard Mr. Morris' voice from down the hall.

"Hello, Aubrey. It's me, Jack Morris."

A smile crossed my lips as I turned my head in the direction in which his voice was coming from.

"Hello, Mr. Morris. How are you?"

"I'm great, young lady. How are you?"

"I'm fine. Thank you for asking. Are you going to see my Aunt Charlotte?"

"I am. We're going to see a show on Broadway tonight."

"Which show are you seeing?"

"*Jersey Boys*. Charlotte expressed an interest in it, so I got us two tickets for tonight."

"I've heard it's very good. Have a good time," I spoke as I opened the door.

"Thanks, kiddo. I'll talk to you soon."

I gave him a small smile before walking into my apartment and shutting the door. After I locked up and put my leftovers in the refrigerator, I went into the bathroom and started the water for a bath. As I was relaxing and soaking up the lavender smell from the few drops of oil I placed in the water, my phone alerted me that I had a text message from Ethan. Drying my hands on the towel next to the tub, I reached over and pressed the message button on my phone as it read to me his text.

"I just wanted to tell you that you looked really beautiful."

A sick feeling in the pit of my stomach emerged and I didn't know what to do. I didn't want to hear that from him. Maybe he felt that since he apologized, it was okay to toy with my emotions. But it wasn't okay and I wasn't going to stand for it anymore. I spent the last couple of days in the hurt phase and now I found myself entering into the angry phase. How dare he say what he did to me. How dare he use me the way he did. I didn't care how broken of a man he was; it didn't give him the right.

"Thank you. But please don't text or call me again. The damage is done, I forgave you, you made yourself perfectly clear on where you stood as far as I was concerned, and now it's time for me to forget that I ever met you."

I waited for a response that never came, which was fine with me. I said what I needed and it was time to close that chapter of my life. Tomorrow, I would start a new chapter; one that didn't involve a man named Ethan Klein.

Chapter 23
Ethan

I sat on the edge of my bed and read her text message. She forgave but she still hated me and I deserved it. When I saw her walking down the street as I exited the restaurant, I couldn't help but smile, because that was what she did to me. Nobody had that kind of power or control over me. Dr. Perry was right; I could feel the control over my emotions and feelings slipping away and it scared the fuck out of me. She wanted to forget she ever met me and after reading that, I felt like I had been stabbed in the heart.

The next morning, I got up from my desk and walked outside my office on my way to the tech department when I noticed Holly wasn't at her desk.

"Lucy, where's Holly?" I asked.

"She's in the bathroom. She's not feeling well."

"What's wrong with her?"

"Morning sickness."

I sighed as I rolled my eyes and headed to the tech department.

"Well?" I asked Rob as I approached his office.

"You gave us three days, Ethan. It's only been two."

"Do you have anything at all?" I asked with irritation.

"We're making some progress. We'll update you tomorrow once we have more. By the way, I'll have the demo glasses ready for you tomorrow."

"Have you tested it out yet?"

"No. We thought we'd let you do the honors." He smiled.

"Wise decision."

Walking back to my office, I noticed Holly still wasn't at her desk.

"Lucy, where's Holly this time?"

"She's back in the bathroom."

Turning around, I went to the women's bathroom and opened the door.

"Holly, are you in here?" I asked.

"Yes, Mr. Klein."

"It seems to me that you spend more time in here than you do at your desk and now I'm seeing this as a problem. You assured me that there wouldn't be a problem."

"I'm sorry, sir." She emerged from the stall, wiping her mouth with a piece of toilet paper.

I stood there shaking my head and stared at the paleness of her face. "Just clean yourself up and get back to work."

I arrived home that night at seven thirty, poured myself a drink, and waited for Dr. Perry to arrive. I stood in front of the painting I purchased, which was still wrapped up and leaning against my wall. As I removed the brown wrapping, I stared at it as I sipped on my drink. Aubrey wasn't the only one who lived in a world of darkness. But I was not so sure that she did. She had found things that put light in her life, regardless if she could see or not.

The doorbell rang and when I walked over and opened it, Dr. Perry was standing there.

"Good evening, Ethan. Are you ready for our session?"

"Hello, Dr. Perry. Yes. Please come in."

I led her to the living room and had her take a seat in my black leather chair while I sat on the couch.

"May I get you something to drink?"

"No. I'm good. So tell me how the past couple of days have been. Did you reach out to Aubrey?"

"I actually saw her last night. I had just finished with a dinner meeting and as I was leaving the restaurant, I saw her walking down the street."

"And?"

"I stopped in front of her and I apologized for the things I said that night and I told her that I didn't mean to hurt her."

"How did she respond?"

"She accepted my apology and then got away from me as fast as she could. I sent her a text message and told her how beautiful she looked. She responded by telling me never to call her again and that it's time she forgot she ever met me."

"Do you blame her?" Dr. Perry asked.

"Not really."

"Aubrey is now protecting herself like you're protecting you. And you can't blame her for that."

"I know."

"What happened with Sophia was a long time ago and I thought you were healing from it. After our last session, you told me you accepted the fact that it wasn't your fault and then I never saw you again."

"Because the nightmares stopped. After two years, they finally stopped."

"Do you know why they stopped?" she asked.

"Not really."

"Because you successfully buried all your emotions and feelings. You became numb, not letting anyone ever get close to you. Unknowingly, you let your guard down with Aubrey. Something about her touched you, and it touched you enough to follow her to Shakespeare Garden that Saturday morning. Maybe it's time, Ethan, to start living life again the way it should be lived. You've suffered and endured enough pain over the past nine years. Sophia had problems way before she met you. You swooped in and tried to save her, but you couldn't. What happened was not your fault. She was already in an altered state of mind from the drugs. It's time you let go."

I watched as she glanced over at the painting.

"What a lovely painting." She got up from her chair and walked over to it. "Who painted it?"

I walked over and stood next to her.

"Aubrey's best friend, Penelope. It was her art exhibition at the gallery the night I met Aubrey. She told me something that night while we were talking about the painting. This was before I knew she was blind. She asked me what I saw when I looked at it. So, I described the painting to her and then she asked me what it meant to me. I told her I didn't know and then she spoke these words: 'Even in a world of darkness, there will always be light.'"

"Is the woman in the painting Aubrey?" she asked as she glanced over at me.

"Yes."

"Why did you buy this painting, Ethan?"

"I don't know." I looked down.

"I think you do. Our time is up." She grabbed her purse and headed towards the door. "Call my office and schedule an appointment for next week. I think weekly sessions for now would be a good idea."

"I will, and thank you for coming here tonight."

"You're welcome. Have a good night, Ethan."

"You too, Dr. Perry."

Chapter 24
Ethan

As I was walking down the stairs, the smell of Belgian waffles put me in a halfway decent mood. I really didn't have time to sit and eat breakfast, but today, I would make an exception.

"Morning, Ingrid," I spoke as I walked into the kitchen and poured a cup of coffee.

"Good morning. Is that safe to say today?"

"Yep, and it's only because I could smell those Belgian waffles all the way upstairs." I smirked.

"Ah, it's good to see you in a better mood."

"Well, I'm really not. But I'm working on it."

She set the plate of waffles down in front of me and I immediately dug into them. As I was enjoying every last bite, my phone rang. It was my mother.

"Hello," I answered.

"Good morning, son. How are you?"

"I'm fine, Mom. How are you?"

"Good. Good. Listen, I'm coming into the city today to do some shopping. How about taking your mom to lunch?"

"I would like that. What time?"

"You tell me. You're the one who has the hectic schedule."

"Why don't you come to my office around twelve thirty and we'll go to that little French restaurant you love."

"Twelve thirty it is. I'll see you then."

"Bye, Mom."

I took the last bite of my waffles and pushed the plate forward.

"Taking your mom to lunch?" Ingrid smiled.

"Yeah."

"How's Aubrey doing, Ethan?"

Even though I never told Ingrid what happened between us, she could sense something had, and she was brave enough to ask.

"Aubrey told me never to call her again. She wants to forget she ever met me." I sighed.

"Oh boy. I'm not even going to ask."

"Good, because I don't really want to talk about it. I'm working on things, Ingrid."

A small smile graced her face as she looked at me.

"I'm happy to hear that."

"I have to get to the office. I'll talk to you later."

"Have a nice lunch with your mom and tell her I said hi."

"I will."

Climbing into the limo, I shut the door. A perplexed look took over Harry's face as he looked at me.

"What?" I asked.

"You didn't slam the door today. That's a good sign."

"Just drive, Harry." I sighed.

He let out a chuckle and pulled away from the curb. When I arrived at the office, I noticed Holly wasn't at her desk.

"Lucy—"

"Bathroom," she spoke without even letting me finish my sentence.

I turned around, headed to the bathroom, and opened the door.

"Holly, are you okay?" I asked.

"I will be, Mr. Klein. I'll be at my desk in a second. I'm sorry."

"Don't rush. Take your time."

I walked back to my office and found Charles sitting at my desk.

"Good morning. Are you into stalking your employees in the bathroom now?" He smirked.

"Very funny. Get out of my chair," I spoke as I set my briefcase down. "Shouldn't you be at work?"

"I had a meeting this morning, so I figured I'd drop by before heading to the office."

"What time was your meeting?" I looked at my watch. "It's only eight o'clock."

"It was at six. It was the only time a new and very wealthy potential client could meet. So, what's going on with you?"

"What do you mean?" I sat down and leaned back in my chair.

"You've been distant lately."

"I've been busy," I spoke as I shuffled some papers on my desk.

"Too busy to tell your best friend what's going on in your life? I mean, come on, Ethan, what's up with Aubrey?"

"She hates me. Told me never to call her again. End of story."

"I see. Nothing new there. A lot of women tell you that all the time. But this time, it's bothering you."

"Not really."

"Come on, Ethan. Jesus Christ, it's me you're talking to. What the fuck is going on in that head of yours?"

"I'm losing control," I spoke through gritted teeth. "I've developed feelings for Aubrey and I can't stop them."

"Bro," he spoke in a low voice. "It's okay. You're human. There's nothing wrong with that."

"I don't do feelings. You know that."

"You used to. But since Sophia, you've closed yourself off to everyone. At first, I understood and figured you'd get over it. But as the years went by, you got worse. Your company became your obsession. It's all you live for and it's not healthy."

"It's the way I like it."

"I'm not buying that bullshit anymore, Ethan. And neither are you. Because if you did, you wouldn't be in such a shit mood 24/7 over a girl you barely know. Now," he got up from his chair, "you know I love you like a brother. We've been through some serious shit together. But I can't stand by you anymore when you're like this. It's time to put the past to rest. There was nothing you could have done, and if you can't accept that, then I no longer feel sorry for you. You've created an image for yourself. Do you really like people calling you The Iceman? Damn it, you can't let one person ruin your entire life and change the man you used to be. I have to go." He shook his head as he walked out the door.

Picking up a pen, I threw it across my desk.

"Excuse me, Mr. Klein," Holly softly spoke as she popped her head through the door.

"Come on in, Holly."

"Umm—" She looked down and folded her hands.

I let out a sigh. "Just say whatever you have to say."

"I have a doctor's appointment first thing Monday morning. I tried really hard to get a later appointment, but they were all booked. So I wanted to ask you if it's okay that I come in a little late? If not, I understand."

I sat there and watched this girl tremble from head to toe before my very eyes. She was scared to death of me and I couldn't blame her, judging from the way I treated her over the past two years.

"It's fine, Holly. Just come in when you can."

"Really?" Her head popped up.

"Of course. Your doctor's appointments are important. I understand."

"Thank you, Mr. Klein." She smiled. "I promise I'll be in right after. It shouldn't take very long," she spoke with excitement.

"You're welcome."

She turned and headed for the door. "Thank you again."

"By the way, if you and your husband are still planning that trip to Hawaii, you can have the time off."

Her face lit up and a wide smile splayed across her face.

"Mr. Klein, are you sure?"

"Yes. You should go celebrate your one-year anniversary in Hawaii. Hopefully, your morning sickness will be over by then."

"I don't know what to say except thank you so much. You have no idea how much this means to me."

"You're welcome." I smiled. "Go call your husband and tell him the good news."

****

I was making my way back to my office after a meeting and Lucy informed me that my mother had called. Pulling my phone from my pocket, I noticed I had two missed calls from her.

"Ethan, I've been trying to get a hold of you."

"I'm sorry, but I was in a meeting. Is everything okay?"

"Yes. I need to change our lunch to dinner. Will that work?"

"Why?"

"I got a late start and just got into the city about a half hour ago. I have a million stores I need to go to, so that should give me plenty of time."

"Dinner is fine. Say, around five o'clock? Where do you want to meet? That French bistro isn't open for dinner."

"I know. Let's meet at Benihana over on West 56th Street. I'm in the mood for some Japanese food."

"Sounds good. I'll see you there."

Chapter 25

Aubrey

"Hey, Aubrey, you ready for our staff meeting?" Ian asked as he walked into my classroom.

"Yep. Gotta love these staff meetings after school."

"To be honest, I'd rather have them after and not before. I'm not trying to get up any earlier than I have to."

I gave him a smile as I took hold of his arm.

"How about we do dinner after our meeting?" he spoke.

"Sure. Where do you want to go?"

"I'm in the mood for Japanese. How about Benihana?"

"Okay. I haven't been there in a while." I smiled.

After our staff meeting, Ian told me that Rigby had sent him a text message saying that his meeting tonight with a client got cancelled.

"Would you mind if Rigby joined us for dinner? I want you to meet him so bad."

"I would like that. I'm dying to meet him."

"Excellent!" he spoke with excitement. "I'll text him now."

It seemed like it took us forever to get to the restaurant because traffic was heavier than usual today. Once we arrived, Ian saw Rigby standing outside waiting for us.

"He's already here and looking as sexy as ever," he spoke as he pulled into a parking space.

Shaking my head, and with a smile, I climbed out of the car and felt a hand wrap around my arm.

"You must be Aubrey. Here, let me help you."

"And you must be Rigby." I grinned. "It's nice to meet you."

"Nice to meet you too. Ian has told me so much about you."

"All good, I hope."

"Nothing but the best."

The hostess took us over to our table and I sat on the end so Ian and Rigby could sit next to each other.

"Weird. We're the only ones at this table so far," Ian spoke.

"It's still early. This place usually doesn't start getting crowded until around six."

"Do you need me to read you the menu?" Rigby politely asked.

I couldn't help but smile at his generosity. "No. I've been here enough that I pretty much know what they have."

"Oh shit," Ian spoke in a low voice.

"What?" I asked.

Before he had a chance to answer, I heard the hostess walking over with other patrons. I inhaled deeply and closed my eyes for a moment as a familiar scent crossed my path.

"Aubrey?" Ethan spoke.

"Aubrey, sweetheart," his mother spoke. "What a surprise seeing you here." She clasped my shoulders and kissed my cheek.

"Hello, Nancy."

"Ethan, you sit here next to Aubrey."

This was the last thing I needed. Oh my God. How was I going to get through this dinner?

"Hello, Ian. Nice to see you again."

"Ethan," he spoke in a disgruntled tone. "This is my friend, Rigby. Rigby, meet Ethan Klein."

"It's nice to meet you, Mr. Klein."

"Likewise, Rigby."

I heard the scraping of the chair across the floor as he pulled it out and took a seat next to me.

"I can request to sit somewhere else," he leaned over and whispered to me.

I wanted to tell him to do it, and if he had been with anyone else besides his mother, I would have.

"It's fine."

My heart was racing a mile a minute as Nancy carried on a conversation with me. More guests were seated and it just so happened that the woman who sat next to Nancy was a girl she knew back in high school. Go figure. That left me and Ethan the odd ones out since everyone else had someone to talk to.

"May I get you a drink?" The waitress with the high-pitched voice asked me.

"I'll have a Mai Tai, please."

"And for you, sir?"

"I'll have a scotch on the rocks. Make it a double."

After she went around the table and took everyone's drink order, we placed our order for dinner.

"How was your day today?" Ethan asked cautiously.

"It was good."

I didn't ask him how his day was because, frankly, I didn't care. Like I said before, I was now in the angry stage.

"I'm surprised you're with your mom," I spoke.

"Why?"

"I just figured you'd be with someone else."

Shit. I really didn't mean to say that.

"No. She was in the city shopping and asked me to have dinner with her. Well, actually, we were supposed to have lunch, but she got a late start."

"That's nice."

"And I'm not seeing anyone else. Why would you say or think that?"

"Because, Mr. Klein, you're a man and you have needs."

"Aubrey, please. Don't do this."

"They were your words, not mine."

"You know what? Maybe it's best if we don't speak," he whispered.

"That's probably for the best."

"I told you that I would switch tables."

"Why are you speaking?"

I heard the sharp intake of his breath and the ice clanking in his glass as he picked it up. We sat there in awkward silence as I sipped on my Mai Tai.

"Listen, you can hate me all you want, but just not right now. My mother doesn't know anything and she'll start asking questions. So please, just for the next hour, at least pretend to hold a conversation with me."

"I have nothing to say to you. So how am I supposed to do that?" I whispered.

"Oh, you two look like you're in deep conversation," Nancy spoke with excitement.

"See. I told you," Ethan whispered. "Well, now we don't have to worry about it; our chef is here."

"I know. I heard him wheel the cart over."

As the chef put on a show and prepared our meal, I sipped on my Mai Tai. I needed to remember the things Ethan said to me because even though I was in my angry stage, his scent was driving me crazy. During dinner, I talked a bit with Ian and Rigby, and Ethan held a conversation with his mother. This had to be the most awkward dinner I was ever at and I couldn't eat fast enough to get the hell out. All I wanted to do was go home, climb into bed, and hide under the covers for the rest of the night.

I finished eating and waited patiently for Ian and Rigby to finish.

"Are you done yet?" I leaned over and asked Ian.

"Yes. We're done," he replied. "Let me ask the waitress for the check."

"No need," Ethan spoke. "Dinner was on me tonight."

"Ethan, that's very kind of you, but we couldn't let you pay," Ian spoke.

"What are you doing?" I whispered in a harsh tone.

"It's only dinner, Aubrey. Now you're free to go."

I didn't want to thank him, but being the good person I was, I had no choice.

"Thank you."

"You're welcome."

I pushed back my chair and as I was about to get up, I felt a hand on mine.

"Let me help you," Ethan spoke as he gently gave my hand a squeeze.

A thousand lightning bolts raced throughout my body as I stood there, frozen for a second, just taking in the touch of his hand on mine. A touch that I hadn't forgotten and didn't think I ever would.

"Thank you." I pulled my hand away.

As soon as we exited the restaurant, Nancy gave me a hug and told me not to be a stranger.

"Have a safe drive home," I spoke as I said goodbye to her.

"Hey, Aubrey," Ian spoke. "Is it okay with you if we stop at Nordstrom? I want to pick up a couple of things and so does Rigby."

"You two go ahead. I'll catch a cab home."

"What? You don't want to come with us?" Ian whined.

"I have some things to do at home and it's been a long day. No worries; you two go and have fun."

"I'll drive you home," Ethan spoke.

"No thank you. I'll catch a cab."

"Don't be ridiculous, Aubrey. Why pay for a cab ride when I can give you a free one?"

Ugh. I was going to kill Ian for putting me in this situation.

"Please. It's just a ride home," he spoke. "And I promise I won't speak to you."

"Fine," I huffed.

"My arm?" Ethan spoke.

"What about it?"

"Are you going to take it?"

"No."

"Oh for god sakes, Aubrey." He grabbed my hand, wrapped it around his arm, and led me to the limo.

Upon opening the door, I slid into the backseat.

"Hello, Aubrey. It's good to see you again."

"Hi, Harry. How are you?"

"I'm good."

I heard the other door open and Ethan slid in next to me.

"Harry, we're driving Aubrey home."

Chapter 26
Ethan

Imagine the shock on my face when I saw Aubrey sitting at the table. She was the last person I expected to run into, let alone sit next to her for dinner. She had an attitude with me and I didn't blame her. I hadn't seen that side of her yet and, to be honest, it turned me on. The car ride back to her apartment was silent because I knew that was the way she wanted it. I was struggling inside. Struggling with the fact that I had hurt her so deeply. Harry pulled up to the curb of her building and I quickly got out and opened the door for her, holding out my hand.

"Please take my hand and let me help you out."

"I don't need help, Ethan. I can get out of a car on my own."

"I know you can, but—"

"Then let me."

When I lowered my hand, she climbed out of the car and placed her cane down in front of her.

"Good night, Ethan."

"Good night, Aubrey."

I watched as she walked inside her building. Clenching my fist as hard as I could, I took in a deep breath, for I knew what I had to do.

"You can have the rest of the night off, Harry. I'll catch a cab home. There's something I need to say to her."

"Good luck, Ethan."

I ran inside the building and placed my hand in between the elevator doors as they began to close.

"Aubrey, I need to talk to you."

"Ethan, what the hell are you doing? I thought you left."

"I can't leave without making things right with you. Please just hear what I have to say."

She stood there in silence, looking down. I knew she was struggling with the decision whether to hear me out or not.

"Please, Aubrey," I spoke in a soft voice.

"Fine. I'll hear you out, but after I do, you are to leave."

"I will. I promise."

We stepped off the elevator, and as soon as we approached her apartment, the door from across the hall opened and a man and woman stepped out.

"Oh, hello, Aubrey," the older woman spoke and then glared at me.

"Hi, Aunt Charlotte. Hello, Mr. Morris."

"Hello, little lady," he spoke.

"Aunt Charlotte, I would like you to meet Ethan Klein. Ethan, this is my Aunt Charlotte and Mr. Morris from apartment 1C."

"It's nice to meet you, Charlotte." I extended my hand.

Her eye narrowed at me as she hesitantly placed her hand in mine without saying a word.

"Nice to meet you, Ethan." Mr. Morris shook my hand.

"Likewise." I smiled.

Aubrey opened her apartment door and we both stepped inside.

"Have fun, you two." She smiled as she closed the door behind her.

"I don't think your aunt likes me too much."

"No. Actually, she doesn't. She heard talk around the city and the things said were not good."

I stood there with my hands in my pockets, lightly nodding my head.

"I deserve that."

Aubrey walked into the living room and took a seat on the couch.

"What did you want to say to me, Ethan? I don't have all night." Her tone was harsh.

I could feel anxiety taking over me, so I took in a long, deep breath. I was nervous as hell because this was something I didn't do.

"May I sit down next to you?" I asked.

"Whatever, Ethan. Just say what you have to say."

I took a seat next to her and swallowed hard while my heart pounded out of my chest.

"I meant to push you away and with everything I said, most of it was the truth. I have rules, Aubrey. Rules about women. I don't stay after because I don't feel anything, so there's no point in leading anyone on. But with you, I wanted to stay and it scared the hell out of me. For the first time in many years, I didn't want to leave after sex. Shortly after Sophia died, I started having nightmares about that night and then they stopped after I was in therapy for a while. Then, the first night I was with you, the nightmares came back. You need to understand that I'm a destroyed man. I've buried every emotion and every feeling I ever had deep down inside me. That's why the nightmares stopped and why I never felt anything for any of the women I was with. Then I met you and, suddenly, things started to resurface and I couldn't control it."

"What things?" she asked.

"It may sound crazy because we haven't known each other very long, but I started to have feelings for you right away, and I did things that I would never do. Every day, I would lose a little more control where you were concerned and I found it difficult to handle. I wanted to push you away, because if I did, then I wouldn't have to feel these things anymore. When you were begging me to stay, it made me angry because I couldn't control the fact that I didn't want to leave."

"What happened the night Sophia died?" she asked.

"Only very few people know what happened that night. My parents don't even know the whole truth."

She reached over and placed her hand on my thigh.

"You can trust me, Ethan. I promise."

"Do you have any liquor? Something stronger than wine?"

"In the upper cabinet above the refrigerator there's a bottle of Jack Daniels. You're more than welcome to have some."

"Thanks."

I got up from the couch, went into the kitchen, and grabbed the bottle of whiskey from the cabinet.

"There are a couple shot glasses in the cabinet next to the stove," she spoke.

After reaching for the glass, I poured myself a shot, kicked it back, and took in the burn as it cascaded down my throat. I poured another and took it back into the living room.

"Sophia and I met when we were eighteen years old at a wedding I had attended for one of my parents' friends. I remember standing there talking to Charles and every time I glanced over at her, she was staring at me. So I walked over, introduced myself, and we spent the rest of the night talking and getting to know each other." I kicked back the shot of whiskey and set the glass down on the coffee table. "I took her out the next night and we had spent every moment we could together for the next three years."

"You must have really loved her," Aubrey spoke.

"I did. I couldn't imagine my life without her. I found out about three months after we were dating that she was using drugs. She told me she only did it occasionally and she promised she'd stop because she knew how I felt about it. Her occasional drug habit eventually turned into a daily one. About a year and a half into our relationship, I finally talked her into getting some help. She checked herself into a rehab facility and got clean."

"What kinds of drugs did she do?"

"Cocaine. She stayed clean for about six months, and those six months were really good for us. Then, her sister was killed in a car accident and she couldn't cope. So, she started using cocaine again along with amphetamines."

"I'm sorry, Ethan, but I have to ask. Why did you stay with her?"

"Because I loved her and I couldn't turn my back on her. She was so screwed up and all she kept telling me was that I was the only stability she had in her life. So I dealt with it the best I could and tried to get her to get clean again. The night she died, we were in California at a friend's birthday party at his beach house. She had been acting weird all day and I kept asking her what was wrong and she insisted nothing. But I could tell something was bothering her. Later that night, I left with Charles and another friend of mine to run to the store to get some more liquor and when I came back, I couldn't find her. When I went upstairs for the third time, she was just coming out of the bathroom. I asked her why she didn't respond to my calling her name and she said she didn't hear me. She was as high as a kite at that point. I walked into the bathroom and found two syringes on the floor. She had just shot herself up with heroin." I swallowed hard. "I'll never forget how I felt at that moment. I was enraged. Anger consumed me so badly that I couldn't see straight. I grabbed the syringes off the floor and flew down the stairs, grabbing her arm and leading her outside away from the party. I asked her when she started shooting up heroin and she told me she'd been doing it for a while. How I didn't know was beyond me."

"Because you loved her and you didn't want to see it. You know how they say love is blind," she spoke.

I stared at Aubrey when she said that and she was right. I had noticed over the past couple of months leading up to her death that she was acting different and changing before my eyes every day.

"I started yelling at her and then I gave her an ultimatum. I told her that it was either the drugs or me and that I'd had enough. I couldn't live like that anymore. She told me that as much as she loved me, she couldn't give up the drugs. So I told her we were over, and as I walked away, she ran after me and grabbed my arm, begging me not to go. I turned to her, took hold of her arms, and begged her to stop the drugs. I told her that I would check her into rehab the next morning and if she wouldn't go, I would walk away. She looked me straight in the eye, and after a few moments of silence, she agreed to go. I held her tight and told her how much I loved her. She asked me if I could go into the house and get her some aspirin and a glass of water. When I came back out, I couldn't find her anywhere. I screamed her name over and over again. It was so dark out except for the lights from the boats in the water out in the distance. A fear came over me and I started to panic as I ran down to the beach and found a trail of her clothes leading to the water. I yelled her name over and over again as I kicked off my shoes, tore off my shirt and ran into the water. Charles and a couple other guys heard me screaming for her and they came running down, asking me what was going on. I couldn't find her, and just like that, she was gone. Charles called 911 and the police were out within a few minutes. The search went on for a few days, but they never did find her body."

Aubrey scooted closer to where I was sitting and placed her hands firmly on my shoulders.

"I'm so sorry, Ethan. I can't even imagine."

"She died because of me. Because of the ultimatum I gave her. Had I never told her that I would leave, she wouldn't have gone into the ocean and killed herself."

"You don't know that. She was messed up from the drugs. What happened to her was not your fault. You have to believe that."

"That's what everyone who knows what happened told me. But in the end, it was my words that led her to the water."

Chapter 27
Aubrey

I reached over and wrapped my arms around him. My heart felt so much sadness as he told his story that it took everything I had not to break down. I now saw him in a different light. He blamed himself for Sophia's death and had been carrying that around with him all these years. I understood all too well about guilt and having the burden of it take over your life. I broke our embrace and placed my hands on each side of his face.

"Thank you for telling me. I know how hard that was for you."

"I wanted you to know why I am the way I am." He removed my hands and held them in his. "After her death, I buried myself into my work, started Klein Technology, and devoted my life to it. I live, eat, and breathe that company. I don't make time for anyone or anything else. I like you, Aubrey. I really do, and I don't want to hurt you anymore. You don't deserve it. All I want is to make love to you more than anything else in the world, but I can't commit to anything and I know you want more."

Even after confessing to me about Sophia, he was still frightened. I wanted to take away his pain, but would I be happy just being a casual fling? Would it be selfish of me to keep having sex with him with the hopes that he'd change his mind down the road? Or would I be setting myself up for an even worse heartbreak? I wasn't that type of person. Or was I? I didn't know because I had never been in a situation like this before. All I knew was, at that moment, I wanted him and he wanted me. He could have gone and had sex with any woman he wanted, but he was here, with me.

Letting go of his hands, I gripped the bottom of my shirt and pulled it over my head. Reaching back, I unhooked my bra and slid it off, tossing it onto the floor. The sharp intake of his breath heighted my excitement as I took his hands and placed them firmly on my breasts.

"Are you sure, Aubrey?" he asked with a whisper.

"Yes."

While one hand firmly gripped my breast, he placed his other hand on my cheek. I could feel the warmth of his breath sweep across my face. Instead of our lips meeting for the first time, his tongue trailed along my neck. It felt so good to be touched by him again. He leaned me back on the couch so I was lying down, and while his mouth made its way to my breasts, his hand slid down my torso and unbuttoned my pants. He sat up and pulled them off and his fingers traced the outline of my lips through the silk fabric of my panties. Before I knew it, his head was buried between my legs and my panties were off in a split second. His mouth wasted no time devouring me as I arched my back, forcing him to go deeper. Subtle moans rumbled in his throat as he explored my opening, flicking his tongue in and out and making small circles around my clit. The pleasure built inside me. He took his fingers and tugged at my hardened nipples as his mouth sent my body into an explosive orgasm. I let out a low moan as my breath escaped me and my heart raced faster than the speed of light.

He didn't speak a word as he sat up and pulled me on top, my knees straddling him. Slowly lowering myself onto his hard cock, I gasped as did he while I took his entire length inside me.

"God, you feel so good," he whispered in my ear.

His hands stayed firmly on my hips as I slowly moved up and down, taking in the moment that I didn't want to end. As much as I was enjoying this, I wanted him to kiss me. I needed to feel his lips on mine, but I wouldn't force it or him. He had his reasons for why he never kissed me. Another orgasm was on its way as I tightened my grip on his shoulders and he tightened his grip on my hips.

"Come for me, baby. I need to feel you come all over my cock," he panted as he thrust his hips and deepened inside me.

Letting out the sound of ecstasy, my body gave in as the rush of warmth over his cock elated him.

"That's it. Oh God. Yes." He strained as he held my hips in place and exploded inside me.

Wrapping my arms around his neck, I laid my head on his shoulder as his arms wrapped around me and held on tight. I prayed that he'd stay the night. I knew it was something he didn't do, but in light of our recent conversation, I hoped he'd change his mind. He stood up, telling me to hold on as he carried me to the bedroom and set me on the edge of the bed. He pulled back the covers and I climbed under them, pulling the sheet up over my naked body. I was a nervous wreck that he was getting ready to leave. But instead, he climbed in on the other side, wrapped his arm around me, and pulled me into him.

"You don't mind if I stay the night, do you?"

My lips gave way to a delighted smile. "I don't mind at all," I replied as I snuggled against him.

We lay there, his hand stroking my hair as my fingers trailed along his chest. I had never felt as safe as I did at that moment.

"How are you feeling?" I asked. "Are you okay?"

"I'm fine, Aubrey. Thank you for listening to me." His lips kissed the top of my head.

"You're welcome. Can I ask you a question?"

"Of course."

"Why won't you kiss me?"

"I've been waiting for you to ask me that." He sighed. "I have a no kissing rule. I can't explain it. It's just something I don't do. I haven't kissed anyone passionately since Sophia. I hope you can understand that."

I lied and told him I did, even though I didn't. There was something between us. I felt it and I knew he did too. I could feel and sense it. Maybe he just needed some time to adjust. After all, he did just tell me about her. I pressed my lips against his chest and then closed my eyes. When I awoke the next morning, I was alone in bed but could smell the freshly brewed coffee coming from the kitchen and I could hear the opening and closing of cabinets. I let out a sigh of relief that he was still here.

"Good morning." I smiled as I tied my robe and walked to the kitchen.

"Good morning. I hope I didn't wake you."

"No. You didn't. What are you doing?"

"I wanted to make us breakfast, but I can't seem to find a pan to cook the eggs in."

I gently smiled and walked over to the cabinet next to the stove. Reaching down, I pulled out the frying pan.

"Is this what you're looking for?"

"Yes. But I swear I looked in that cabinet."

"Go sit down. I'll make breakfast."

"Oh no you don't. I'm cooking. So go sit down and I'll get you a cup of coffee," he insisted.

"Seriously, Ethan—"

Before I knew it, his hands were grasping my shoulders.

"Go sit down. I'm cooking breakfast. End of discussion. Do you understand?" He led me to the barstool at the counter.

"Fine. I'll sit down."

"Thank you. Now, how do you like your eggs?"

"Scrambled is fine."

He set a cup of coffee down in front of me and told me to be careful.

"It's hot. Don't burn yourself."

"Yes, Ethan. I know it's hot. But I will be extra careful for you." I smirked.

"You're a little snippy from time to time. Do you know that?"

"Only when someone insists on treating me like a handicapped child."

"I'm sorry. I'm learning."

"I know you are. Just make my eggs. I'm starving."

"What are your plans for today?" he asked.

"I don't know. I really don't have any."

"After I make breakfast, I'm going to go home, shower, change, and head to the office. I have quite a bit of work to do."

"It's Saturday."

"Saturdays are no different from any other day of the week as far as I'm concerned."

I sat there, sipping my coffee with the hopes that he'd want to spend the day together. I needed to play it off as if I didn't care.

"Sounds boring." I smirked.

He chuckled. "It can be."

After we finished breakfast, he cleaned up the kitchen and then kissed me on my forehead.

"Enjoy your day. I have to go."

"You too. Try not to work too hard."

"I can't make any promises."

He walked out the door and I sighed. I wasn't sure I could do this.

Chapter 28
Ethan

I hailed a cab home and got ready for work. As I stood in the shower, I lowered my head and let the water beat down on me while I thought about Aubrey. For the first time in years, I felt like a weight had been lifted from my shoulders. Telling her about Sophia and making her understand the way I was, was gratifying. I was honest and told her I couldn't commit to anything and yet she still wanted to make love. Which to me, was a sign that she was okay with it. I still had fears, and many of them. Would I ever go back to the way I was? I didn't know. But, little by little, Aubrey was peeling away the damaged layers that resided inside me. Spending the night with her was great and I didn't feel like I needed to leave. It was the least I could do for her since she sat and listened to what I had to say. Did this mean we were in a relationship? No. It meant that we reached a level where we could enjoy each other's company without any strings attached.

As I was sitting in my office doing some work, a text message came through from her.

"Hey, I know you're busy working, but I'm going rock climbing today and wanted to see if you wanted to tag along. It'll be fun."

Rock climbing? Was she serious? She couldn't rock climb. A nervousness settled inside me at the thought. She'd slip and fall and possibly get killed. All sorts of things ran through my head.

"Is anyone going with you?"

"Nope. Just me and you if you want to come along."

Damn it. There was no way I could let her go alone.

"What time are you going and where are you going?"

"Three o'clock at Chelsea Pier Sports Center. I have a friend who works there."

I let out a sigh of relief. She was going to go to a gym to rock climb. That made me feel somewhat better because someone would be there with her.

"I really can't. I'm sorry. I have so much to do."

"That's fine. I just thought I'd ask."

I set down my phone and got back to work. My tech team was working today on that app I wanted to create. Walking down to their department, I found them huddled around a table.

"Anything yet?" I asked.

"We're having trouble with the voice over. It's thirty percent complete."

"Alright. Just keep working at it."

Looking at my watch, I noticed it was three o'clock. Why on earth would she want to rock climb? Fuck. I couldn't get the thought out of my head. Instead of going back to my office, I headed out the door and hailed a cab to the Chelsea Pier Sports Center.

When I arrived, I asked the young attractive girl at the front desk where their rock climbing was.

"All the way in the back and to the right. Do you have an appointment?" she asked.

"No. I'm just here to support a friend of mine who's doing it."

"Oh. Okay."

When I found the section where the rock climbing was, I clenched my fist when I saw a man with his arms around Aubrey's waist. I stood back and watched as she began to climb the wall. The man who had helped her glanced over and looked at me. Bringing my finger to my lips, I motioned for him not to alert Aubrey that I was there.

"Hey, Alyssa, keep an eye on Aubrey. I'll be right back."

He walked over to me and we stepped away from the area.

"Can I help you with something?"

"I'm just here to watch her, but I don't want her to know."

"Dude, that's creepy."

I couldn't help but give him a half smile.

"I'm a close friend of hers. She called me earlier and asked me to come with her, but I couldn't. I just wanted to see her do it. To be honest, I'm a little nervous."

"Why? It's not the first time she's rock climbed. She's been here several times and she's really good. If you're such a close friend, you would know that. Listen, you need to let her know you're here or I'm going to have to ask you to leave. Then, after you leave, I'll tell her you were here but didn't want her to know."

"Fine."

"What's your name?" he asked.

"Ethan Klein."

"I'm Justin. Nice to meet you."

Rolling my eyes, I followed him over to where Aubrey was. She was already halfway up the wall.

"Hey, Aubrey," Justin spoke.

"Yeah." She turned her head to him.

"You have a visitor. He says his name is Ethan Klein."

"Ethan." A smile crossed her face. "I thought you couldn't come."

"I finished earlier than I thought, so I came down here to watch you."

"Watch me? No, Ethan, I want you to climb with me."

"I can't, Aubrey. I don't have the right clothes or anything. I'll do it another time."

"Promise?" she asked with a smile.

"I promise."

She finished climbing and came back down the wall. Even though she was a sweaty mess, she looked incredible.

"Great job, Aubrey," Justin spoke. "See you next week?"

"Thanks, Justin. I'll be here."

I took her hand and placed it on my arm.

"I didn't know you rock climbed," I spoke as we headed out the door.

"There's a lot you don't know about me."

I smiled. "Is that so? Then how about we have dinner tonight and you can tell me more about the things I don't know about you."

"As much as I would love to, I can't. I'm having dinner and drinks with Penelope and my Aunt Charlotte."

"Ah. Okay. Maybe I can see you after?"

"I'm not sure what time I'll be home. Since we're hitting the town, I probably won't be getting in until really late."

"Okay. I understand. How about we share a cab?"

"I'd like that. No Harry today?"

"Nah. He went out of town for the weekend."

I hailed us a cab and we climbed into the backseat.

"Why didn't you drive your car?" She smirked.

"I didn't feel like dealing with the traffic."

She let out a light laugh. "Even though I have never actually seen what the traffic looks like in New York City, I can sure feel it, so I understand."

"We have arrived at your apartment. Would you like me to come up for a while?" I asked.

"As much as I'd like that, I have to shower and get ready, so I won't be much company."

"Oh. Okay. Have a good time with Penelope and your aunt."

"Thanks, Ethan. Enjoy your evening." She climbed out and shut the door.

Chapter 29

Aubrey

I knew what I was doing. He couldn't commit, so neither could I. I wasn't about to sit around waiting for him to call me whenever the mood struck him.

"So you're playing hard to get?" my Aunt Charlotte asked as she sipped her wine.

"Pretty much."

"Eeek! I'm so proud of you." Penelope placed her hand on mine.

"He wants to have a relationship with me, just not a dating one."

"Well, you know that I find that extremely hot in a man. They secretly want you but can't let you know because of their issues," Penelope spoke. "Just fuck him and leave him hanging."

"Penelope!" Aunt Charlotte exclaimed.

"What? He does it. In fact, a lot of men do it. So there's no reason why my best friend can't do it too. She's not a damn doormat. Guys just can't walk all over her, wipe their feet, walk away, and then come back when their shoes are dirty again."

"What?" Aunt Charlotte sighed. "Listen, Aubrey. You know how I feel about that man."

"I know, Aunt Charlotte, but you don't have to worry. He is a good man. I knew it the minute I met him, to be honest. He just has some issues he needs to work out before he can move on with his life. Our conversation last night proved it."

"So what did happen to his girlfriend?" Penelope asked.

"She drowned in the ocean and he loved her very much. He's still dealing with that loss."

"I don't know, Aubrey," my Aunt Charlotte spoke.

"Trust me." I reached over and grabbed her hand. "He's a good man."

****

The next morning, I was awoken by the sound of my phone letting me know that Ethan was calling.

"Hello," I sleepily answered.

"Did I wake you?"

"Oh no. I was just lying here," I lied. "What time is it anyway?"

"It's eight o'clock and I'm sorry. I did wake you."

"I had to get up anyway."

"How would you like to go with me to the Hamptons today?"

A smile crossed my face. "I'd like that."

"Good. I was hoping you'd say yes. Charles and Lexi are heading there to spend the day on the boat. They invited me and asked me to ask you."

"Sounds fun."

"How fast can you be ready?"

"Umm. An hour? When did you want to come pick me up?"

"Well, I'm standing outside your door."

"What?" I laughed. "I'm hanging up and I will be there in a second to let you in."

Climbing out of bed, I slipped on my robe and walked to the front door, unlocking it and letting Ethan in.

"Good morning." He kissed my forehead.

"Good morning." I smiled.

"You go get ready and I'll make you some coffee."

"Thank you. I won't take too long. I promise."

Making my way into the bathroom, I hopped into the shower and quickly washed my hair. Spending the day with Ethan was going to be perfect and it made me happy that he asked. Climbing out of the shower, I grabbed my towel and wrapped it around me. I could hear his footsteps approaching the bathroom.

"Here's your coffee." He took my hand and placed the cup in it.

"Thanks."

"I brought you something to wear."

"You did?" I asked as I took a sip of my coffee.

"I brought that dress I bought you at Bloomingdales. I thought you might like to wear it on the boat."

"I'd like that." I smiled.

"What time did you get in last night?" he asked.

"Around one."

"Wow. The three of you must have been having a good time."

"We did. We ate, drank, talked. It was fun." I smiled. "What did you do last night?"

"Charles came over. We watched some football, drank a few beers, and ordered a pizza."

I let out a light laugh.

"What?" he asked.

"I just can't imagine you eating pizza and watching football."

"Why? I happen to like football and pizza."

"I don't know. Maybe it's because you're filthy rich."

He chuckled. "And rich people aren't supposed to like sports and pizza?"

"That's not what I'm saying."

"Then what are you saying?" he whispered as he clasped my shoulders and nipped at my ear.

Turning to face him, I wrapped my arms around his neck.

"You're supposed to like golf, polo, and horseracing."

"I like those things too. But I do enjoy a good game of football."

Suddenly, my towel fell off and dropped to the floor.

"Oh, look at that. Your towel fell off," he spoke as his fingers traced over my breasts.

"I thought you were in a hurry to leave." I smiled as his tongue caressed my neck.

"I think we can spare a few moments." He turned me around and took me from behind.

After we finished, he handed me my dress.

"I need some panties."

"Actually, you don't."

"What do you mean, I don't?" I laughed.

"You don't need any. I would prefer it if you didn't wear any under that dress."

"You're a bad boy, Mr. Klein."

"I know." He kissed my forehead. "Okay, now you have fifteen minutes to do your hair so we can get out of here."

After brushing out and blow drying my hair, I threw it up in a ponytail. Grabbing my sandals from the closet, I walked out into the living room, where I heard Ethan talking on the phone.

"Who were you talking to?" I asked as I slipped on my shoes.

"Charles. Unfortunately, he and Lexi aren't going to be able to make it. She's sick."

"Oh. I hope she's okay."

"She thinks it's food poisoning. But we're still going to go."

"Just the two of us?" I grinned.

"Yes. Just the two of us. Charles rented the boat for the day, so I told him that I'd pay him for it since we're going to be using it. Are you ready?"

"I am." I grabbed my purse and my cane.

Chapter 30
Ethan

Getting to spend the day with Aubrey was something I looked forward to doing. After dropping her off at her apartment yesterday afternoon, and knowing that she was going out for the night, set me in a mood. I wanted to spend the rest of the day and evening with her. It was a feeling that completely took over me and I couldn't get her out of my head.

When Charles came over, we had a long talk and he was pleasantly surprised that I told her about Sophia. He said that right there alone was a step in the right direction. And the more I thought about it, he was right. I told her that I couldn't give her more of me. She seemed okay with it, but for me, it felt unsettled. I wanted to change the person I'd become.

We arrived at the marina and I led her onto the boat.

"Good afternoon. I'm Jacque, and I'll be your captain for the day."

"Good afternoon. I'm Ethan Klein and this is Aubrey Callahan. It will only be the two of us today. Charles and his fiancée were unable to make it."

"Okay. If you'd like to explore the boat, be my guest. Up on the deck, you will find some champagne, a large cheese tray, and fresh fruit waiting for you."

"Thank you, Jacque."

Aubrey took hold of my arm and I led her up to the sun deck, where she took a seat on the long blue and white striped couch.

"This is comfy." She smiled.

"Would you like some champagne?" I asked.

"I'd love some."

"Right in front of you, on the table, is the cheese and fruit tray," I spoke.

"Thank you."

I handed her a glass of champagne, sat down next to her, and pulled her into me as her legs sprawled out on the couch and her head pressed against my chest.

"You don't get seasick, do you?" I asked.

"I don't know. I've never been on a boat."

"Well, if you do, let me know. They have medicine here you can take."

Sitting there with my arms wrapped tightly around her felt right. I had so many thoughts running through my head that I needed to have a talk with her.

"There's something I need to talk to you about," I spoke with nervousness.

"Okay." She softly stroked my arm.

"First of all, I need you to turn around and face me."

She set her champagne glass on the table and shifted her body so she was sitting up facing me.

"This sounds serious."

I brought the back of my hand up to her face and softly stroked her cheek.

"I know I told you this the other night, but I'm going to say it again. I really like you, Aubrey, and I like spending time with you. And not just for sex either. I mean, I love having sex with you. You make me feel different, but you also make me feel different just spending time alone with you doing things like this. I know I said that I couldn't commit to anything, but I want to try. You've unraveled me to the point that if I don't see you every day, I could possibly go insane."

She let out a light laugh.

"I want me and you to merge together and become an us. That's if you want the same thing. If you're not ready or think it's too soon, I'll understand. I'm slowly changing because of you, Aubrey Callahan."

"Oh, Ethan." Her eyes filled with tears. "I would love to become an us." She brought her hand up to my face.

"Are you sure? I'm a hard man to be around sometimes. You have to be really sure, because once you're completely mine, I don't think I could ever let you go."

A smile graced her beautiful face. "I'm positive. I want to be all yours and I want you to be all mine."

After tracing her lips with my thumb, I leaned in and softly pressed mine against them. Pulling back, I stared at the smile on her face.

"I need you to do that some more."

"It would be my pleasure."

Cupping her face in my hands, I kissed her passionately and she tasted exactly how I knew she would. Sweet and full of innocence. Our tongues introduced themselves as our kiss deepened. The emotional connection I felt at that moment was unlike anything I'd ever felt before. My cock was at full attention, as was my mind. I was happy again and I owed it all to this beautiful, blonde-haired woman.

Breaking our kiss, she ran her hands down my shirt.

"What am I?" She smiled.

"You, Aubrey Callahan, are my girlfriend."

"And you, Ethan Klein, are my boyfriend."

I pulled her into me and held her tight.

"I'm not sure your aunt is going to be too happy about this."

"Don't worry about Aunt Charlotte. She'll be fine."

We sailed for a few hours, had dinner on the boat, and when we docked, we headed back to New York City.

"I'm spending the night at your place, so we'll stop at my house so I can grab some things and go straight to the office in the morning."

"Good. I was hoping you'd stay with me tonight."

****

The next morning, Ian knocked on the door and Aubrey asked me to answer it since she was still getting ready. Both of us were running late thanks to our little sex session we had this morning.

"Good morning, Ian." I smiled as I opened the door.

"Umm. Hey, Ethan." His eye narrowed at me in confusion. "Did you stay the night?"

"I did. Aubrey said she'll be ready in a second."

"So am I to assume things are good between the two of you?"

"Things are very good. I'm sure she'll tell you all about it on the ride to school." I winked.

Walking back into the bedroom, I kissed Aubrey goodbye.

"Have a good day, sweetheart. I'll see you later."

"You too. I'll miss you."

"I'll miss you too."

Walking out the door, I climbed into the limo and Harry turned around with a grin across his face.

"Well?"

"Miss Callahan and I are dating and you will be seeing her a lot."

"Very good, Ethan. I'm happy for you, my friend."

"Thanks, Harry."

Walking down the hallway to my office, I stopped at Lucy's desk.

"Good morning, Lucy. How was your weekend?"

"Good morning, Mr. Klein. It was good. And yours?" she asked with suspicion.

"It was fantastic. Holly has a doctor's appointment this morning. Send her in my office when she comes in."

"I will."

"Oh, and could you please get me a cup of coffee?"

"I'll bring it right in, sir."

"Thank you." I smiled as I tapped my finger on her desk.

****

Lucy

What the hell was that? I thought to myself as he walked into his office. Getting up from my desk, I went into the break room, poured him a cup of coffee, and took it into his office.

"Here you go, Mr. Klein."

"Thank you, Lucy." He smiled. "Do me a favor and get the product development team up here for a quick meeting."

"I'll call down right now."

Going back to my desk, I picked up the phone and called Rob.

"What's up, Lucy?" he answered.

"Mr. Klein would like you and the team to come up to his office."

"Shit. Right now?"

"Yes. Something's going on with him. He's in a really good mood and, to be honest, I'm scared."

"He's never in a good mood. What's that about?"

"I have no clue."

"We'll be up in a minute."

As I hung up the phone, Holly walked in and set her purse down at her desk.

"Mr. Klein asked to see you when you arrived."

"He did remember I had a doctor's appointment, right?"

"Yeah, and he's in a really good mood. He said good morning to me, tapped his finger on my desk, and said thank you."

"What? What's wrong with him?"

"I don't know, but I'm a little freaked out by it. His mood may not last too much longer, so you better get in there quick."

She took in a deep breath and went into his office. After a few moments, she walked back out with a look of confusion on her face.

"What? What did he say?" I asked with anticipation.

"He asked me how my appointment went and if I was feeling okay. He told me not to worry about my future appointments and if I need to make them in the mornings, I can."

"Weird. Something is going on with that man."

"Yeah and we better take advantage of it while we can." She smirked.

Chapter 31
Aubrey

It had been a month since Ethan and I started officially dating. We traveled back and forth between my apartment and his townhouse. I had gotten to know Ingrid and fell in love with her right away. My Aunt Charlotte was not thrilled when I first told her about us, but the more Ethan was around and the more she got to know him and saw how happy he made me, the easier it was for her to accept him.

Waking up to him every morning was the highlight of my day. Those three little words had yet to escape both of our lips. I loved him and I was sure he loved me. He just hadn't said it and I wasn't going to push him. He hadn't had a nightmare since we'd been together, which was a good thing. Dr. Perry told him that since he let his emotions and feelings for me come full force, the pain he carried around all these years about Sophia began to slowly fade away. The sweetest thing he had done for me was his company created an app that would help visually impaired people navigate their way through large buildings. It was amazing and I was the first one to test it out. Ethan was not only happy that it helped me significantly, he was also happy because Apple paid his company millions of dollars for it.

As I was sipping my morning coffee, Ethan walked over to me and gave me a hug and kiss goodbye.

"My flight doesn't get in until nine o'clock tonight. I'll come right here from the airport."

"Okay. Have a safe trip."

"Oh, before I go, I have something for you." He handed me a small box with a bow tied around it.

"What's this?" I smiled.

"Open it and find out."

After untying the ribbon, I removed the lid from the box and took out what was inside, feeling the fabric in my hands.

"Is this something sexy?" I grinned.

"Yes, and when I get home tonight, I expect you to be wearing it for me."

"It would be my pleasure, Mr. Klein." I reached up and kissed his lips.

"Oh, you're going to be getting a lot of pleasure when I get back. I have to run, baby." He kissed me one last time before walking out the door.

****

Ethan

I had a meeting with Dr. Marchetti at Massachusetts General Hospital, the head and lead surgeon of their ophthalmology department. He was the best in the world and had agreed to meet with me regarding Aubrey.

"Welcome, Mr. Klein. Please have a seat."

"Thank you, and please, call me Ethan."

"What can I do for you, Ethan?" he asked as he took a seat behind his desk.

"I heard about your breakthrough in being able to restore a blind person's eyesight."

"Yes. We have had some success. May I ask why you're asking?"

"My girlfriend lost her eyesight from a car accident when she was eight years old, and she's been permanently blind ever since."

"How old is she now?"

"She's twenty-five."

"Hmm. Do you know what caused it? Brain trauma or direct impact to the eyes?"

"To be honest, I don't know. I came to you with the hope that you might be able to help her see again."

"In order to answer that, I'll need to view her medical file from the accident, and for that I'll need her written consent."

"She doesn't know I'm here. I didn't want to get her hopes up if there wasn't a possibility you could help her.

"I see. And you say this happened seventeen years ago?"

"Yes."

"Let me do some research and I'll give you a call. There are a couple of possibilities as to why she lost her sight after the accident."

Getting up from my chair, I extended my hand. "Thank you, Dr. Marchetti."

"No problem, Ethan." He lightly shook my hand. "Talk to your girlfriend about this and have her sign a form so I can get her medical records. With today's technology, I'm sure we'd be able to help her. I'll be in touch in a couple of days."

"Thank you. I look forward to hearing from you."

****

I arrived at Aubrey's apartment a little after ten o'clock. Inserting my key, I opened the door and headed straight to the bedroom. I had been thinking about her all day in that black nightie with the matching silk string panties. She was going to look delicious in it and I couldn't wait to devour every inch of her.

I had my reasons for contacting Dr. Marchetti. One of them being if there was chance Aubrey could get her eyesight back, that would be incredible for her. I wanted nothing more than for her to be able to see the world as an adult and to also see me. Even though I hadn't told her that I loved her yet, I did. And to be honest, I didn't really know why I hadn't. To me, it was the final commitment in our relationship. I mean, I was one hundred percent committed to her, but there was still a fear inside me that was holding me back.

Walking into the bedroom, I found her lying on her side, hand on her cheek and a smile on her face. She looked so sexy that instantly, my cock rose to the occasion without warning.

"It's about time you got home," she spoke.

After removing my tie, I unbuttoned my shirt and slid it off. As I walked slowly towards the bed, I kicked off my shoes, then unbuttoned my pants and slid them down.

"I missed you." I climbed on the bed and kissed her lips.

"I missed you too. How was your trip?"

"We can talk about that later. We have other business to attend to first."

She lay on her back as my fingers traced the outline of her cleavage first before traveling down the silk fabric of her nightie and reaching the top of her panties. She gasped as my hand slid down the front of her and to her slick lips that were already drenched with pleasure. Dipping my fingers inside her, she gasped and I kissed her mouth softly, nipping at her bottom lip, and teasing her while I explored her insides. I needed to go down on her. Nothing gave me more satisfaction than tasting the sweetness of excitement that emerged from her. I pushed up the silk fabric of her nightie slightly and let my tongue explore her torso, kissing and licking every inch of it. Climbing off the bed, I got down on my knees and lightly pulled her towards me. Hooking my fingers into the sides of her panties, I slid them down and delicately touched her while I licked up her inner thigh. The soft moans that escaped her and the trembling of her skin under my touch had me wanting to explode.

My tongue made its way up her thigh, over her lips, and to her already swollen clit that was begging to be caressed by the tip of my tongue. With each flick, she let out soft sounds of pleasure that heightened when my finger dipped inside her. Grasping the comforter with her hands, her body tightened as she orgasmed. Climbing on top of her, I placed my cock at her entrance and thrust inside as I could no longer wait. Being inside her was what I had waited for all day. I stared into her eyes as I moved rapidly in and out of her, my cock coated with her wetness. There was nothing I wanted more than to have her eyes look into mine and see me. To see the expression on my face as I made love to her, talked to her, and how I reacted when she walked into a room. I wanted her to see how I looked at her every day and how she made me smile.

The buildup had come as I thrust in and out. She was ready to come with me and that made me a happy man.

"Come with me, baby," I panted.

Her legs tightened themselves around my waist as I felt her orgasm, making my cock explode inside her. I leaned down and passionately kissed her before collapsing down to regain my breath and calm my racing heart. Rolling off and onto my side, I ran my hand through her hair.

"Whew. Are you okay?" I asked.

"I'm great." She smiled as we scooted off the bed and climbed under the sheets.

I pulled her tightly into me and kissed the top of her head. I was exhausted but not too exhausted to talk to her. We lay there in silence for a moment, me softly stroking her arm and her lightly running her hand across my chest as her head lay against it.

"Do you ever wish you could see again?" I asked.

"Sometimes. Why do you ask?"

"I just wondered if you ever thought about it. I mean, isn't it something all visually impaired people think about?"

"I'm sure they do. It would be nice to see the ocean, to see the blue sky again, and to actually see what snow looks like."

"Believe me, that shit is best unseen." I chuckled.

She giggled and then said something that really hit my heart hard.

"Sometimes when I know I'm facing a mirror, like when I dry my hair or put on my makeup, I'll just stand there, and even though everything in my world is black, I wish I could see what I look like now that I'm an adult."

"You're beautiful, Aubrey. In fact, you're the most beautiful woman I've ever laid eyes on."

"Ethan. I do believe you may be a little biased since I'm your girlfriend."

"No, sweetheart. I thought that when I first saw you in the art gallery. When I turned around and saw you standing there, I was mesmerized."

Her lips pressed firmly against my chest.

"Thank you."

I tightened my grip around her. Now that I got that question out of the way, I could relax a little. I had no doubt that if Dr. Marchetti could help her, she'd jump at the chance to let him.

Chapter 32
Ethan

A few days had passed and I was a little concerned that I hadn't heard from Dr. Marchetti. I couldn't stop thinking about the possibility of Aubrey getting her sight back. As I was on my way back from an important meeting, my phone rang. Pulling it from my pocket, I noticed it was Dr. Marchetti. I took in a deep breath before answering his call.

"Ethan Klein."

"Ethan, it's Dr. Marchetti over at Massachusetts General. How are you?"

"I'm good, Dr. Marchetti."

"Listen, have you talked to Aubrey about signing over her medical records? I believe there may be something I can do to help her regain her sight. I've done some research and if what happened to her is what I think happened, I am certain I can help her."

I swallowed hard because I couldn't believe it.

"That's wonderful news. I haven't talked to her about it yet, but I will tonight."

"If she agrees, let me know as soon as possible. I will be in New York on Thursday hosting a seminar over at New York Presbyterian University Hospital and could meet with the two of you after."

"That would be great. I'm sure she will agree to it. Just let me know what time."

"The seminar runs until three o'clock. So how about three thirty?"

"We'll be there. Thank you, Dr. Marchetti."

"You're welcome, Ethan, and I'm looking forward to meeting Aubrey."

I ended the call and sat at my desk with a smile on my face. Hearing the door open, I looked up to see Charles walking in.

"What's that smile for?" He grinned.

"Just got some good news."

"Ah. Do tell, my friend." He took a seat across from my desk.

"Remember when I went out to Boston on a business trip last week?"

"Yeah."

"It wasn't really a business trip. I met with a Dr. Marchetti to talk about possibly having Aubrey's eyesight restored."

"What? Are you serious?"

"Very. I just got off the phone with him and he thinks he can help her."

"Wow. That's amazing. I bet Aubrey is ecstatic."

I sighed. "She doesn't know anything about this."

"Say what? You didn't tell her you met with him?"

"No."

"Bro, she's your girlfriend and this involves her. Why the hell wouldn't you tell her?"

"Because I didn't want to get her hopes up until I was sure that he could possibly help her. I'm going to tell her tonight."

"Any idea how she's going to react with you going behind her back like that?"

I rolled my eyes. "I didn't go behind her back."

"Yes, you really did. You met with a doctor about her without her knowing. That's going behind her back, bro."

"She'll be okay with it. I'm not worried."

"I hope so. Anyway, I came to see if you wanted to hit up that burger joint down the street for lunch."

"Sure. Let's go." I grabbed my phone and got up from my desk.

****

Aubrey

I loved my job and I loved my students. Teaching them about English literature was the best part of my life, as well as loving Ethan. I was so happy and life was grand. When I walked through the door of my apartment, his scent was filtering through the air.

"You're here early?" I smiled.

"I had a meeting not too far from here, so I just decided not to go back to the office." He wrapped his arms around me and gave me a kiss. "I missed you."

"I missed you too."

"How about we order something in for dinner. There's something I need to talk to you about."

"Okay. Is everything good?" I asked with concern.

"Everything is good, sweetheart. I promise."

"Since we're staying in, I'm going to take a quick shower."

"Okay. I'll pour us some wine and we can decide what we want to order when you're finished." He kissed my lips once again.

As I stepped into the shower, I was curious as to what he wanted to talk to me about. Maybe he wanted to take a vacation and go somewhere. God, how I would love to go somewhere with him. Like a tropical island where it was just the two of us. A smile crossed my face the more I thought about it. I bet that was it. He wanted to go away somewhere.

After I was finished, I slipped into a pair of sweatpants and a tank top. Removing the towel from my head, I ran a brush through my long hair. Ethan came up from behind me, took the brush out of my hand, and started brushing my hair.

"Here, let me."

"What did you want to order?" I asked.

"Anything you want, sweetheart."

"How about pasta from Luigi's? I've been craving their bread."

"Pasta sounds good." He set down the brush and turned me around so I was facing him. "You're so beautiful and I'm a very lucky man to have you in my life."

"I'm a lucky woman to have you in my life." I hugged him tightly.

He called in our dinner order as I took my wine and sat down on the couch. I was in anticipation of what he wanted to talk to me about and I couldn't wait any longer.

"So what did you want to talk to me about?" I smiled.

"We'll discuss it after dinner. It'll be here soon."

I heard his phone ring.

"Excuse me for a moment. It's the office."

While I sipped on my wine, there was a knock on the door. As I got up to answer it, Ethan ended his call and beat me to the door. Opening up the cabinet, I took down two plates and grabbed some silverware from the drawer, taking them to the table and setting them down.

"Sit down. I've got this."

"Yes, sir." I saluted him.

He let out a chuckle.

"The pasta is to your left and the salad is to your right."

"And the bread?" I asked as I arched my brow.

"Shit. They didn't give us any. I'm sorry, sweetheart."

"Very funny, Ethan." I smiled. "I can smell it."

"I should know better by now, right?"

"Right."

We enjoyed our dinner and talked about our day. Ethan helped me clean up and then poured me another glass of wine.

"Let's go over to the couch, shall we?"

"Okay."

The suspense was killing me. I wondered where he was going to take me. It didn't matter, though. As long as it was just the two of us, I'd be happy anywhere. As we both sat down, I heard him take in a long deep breath.

"Remember how I went to Boston last week?" he asked.

"Of course." I smiled.

"I didn't go there for business."

"You didn't?" I cocked my head.

"No."

"Then why did you go?"

"I met with a doctor. His name is Dr. Marchetti and he's a world renowned eye specialist."

Suddenly, my stomach dropped.

"Why did you meet with him?"

"I wanted to know if there was any way he could help you regain your eyesight. He just needs your permission to access your medical records from the accident, but he believes he can restore your vision. He took the wine glass from me, set it down, and grabbed both of my hands. “He said he wants to meet you on Thursday. He’ll be here in New York hosting a seminar.”

I sat there, my heart beating out of my chest. I couldn’t believe what he had just told me.

“Why would you do something like that without talking to me about it first?”

“Because I didn’t want to get your hopes up if he couldn’t help you.”

I was in shock that he would do something like that without talking to me.

“Aren’t you happy? Aubrey, sweetheart, there’s a chance you could get your eyesight back.”

I pulled away from him and got up from the couch. A feeling of discontent washed over me, not to mention an anger that ripped through my body at what he had done.

“You had no right, Ethan. No right at all. This is my life. Not yours,” I sternly spoke.

“Aubrey, I know it’s your life and I’m trying to help you.”

“I don’t need help. I’m happy with my life the way it is!” I raised my voice.

“Don’t you want to see again? You said the other night that you wished you could see the ocean like you used to, the blue sky, and yourself. My God, sweetheart, if Dr. Marchetti can help you, you could see the world.”

“No. I don’t want to see. This has been my life for more years than I was born. I’m comfortable this way. You just can’t do that, Ethan. FUCK!" I yelled as I placed my hands on my head. "You just can't go messing with people's lives."

"Aubrey, calm down." I felt the firm grip of his hands around my arms.

"Don't, Ethan." I jerked away.

"I thought I was doing something good here. Why can't you understand that? And to be honest, I don't get why on earth you wouldn't want to get your sight back!" he yelled.

"Because that's for me to decide! Not you! And I suspect you want it for your own selfish reasons!"

"I want this for you, Aubrey!" he shouted. "I want this for us!"

"Us? I thought my being blind didn't bother you. So all this time, you were lying to me? You're no different than any other guy out there!"

"Seriously? Your blindness doesn't bother me at all. If it did, I wouldn't be with you."

"Obviously it does or else you wouldn't have sought out that doctor! Just get out of here, Ethan. I don't want to see you right now."

"You don't want to see me? Guess what, Aubrey? You can't see me!" He shouted so loudly that I flinched. "Is it so wrong that I would do and give anything to have you see me? To see the way I look at you, to see my smile and to see how much I fucking love you! Maybe I am being selfish because I want you to see me and see what I look like. Why live in a world of darkness if you don't have to?"

"Because it's the only world I know!" I shouted back.

"It's not the only world you know, Aubrey. You've seen things before the accident and you were forced to adapt into a world only people who are blind can understand. I'm giving you the opportunity to go back to that other world!"

The next set of words flew out of my mouth faster than I could stop them. They were out of anger because he didn't understand.

"I'm not Sophia, Ethan. I don't need saving! You can't save me just like you couldn't save her."

There were a few moments of silence between us. I could just imagine the angry look on his face. The same look that my father had before the crash. I swallowed hard as the tears started to fall down my face.

"That was a low blow, Aubrey."

"Get out," I whispered in a low voice.

"I'm leaving and I don't know when or if I'll be back."

"Don't bother."

"Fine. Then it's over. I thought I was doing something good. But apparently, I'm just a selfish bastard. Good luck to you, Aubrey." I heard the door slam shut.

Falling to my knees, I held my face in my hands and sobbed. A few moments later, the door opened and I heard my Aunt Charlotte's voice.

"Oh my God, Aubrey. What happened?"

She wrapped her arms around me as I cried hysterically into her.

"It's okay, baby. Tell me what happened."

I couldn't talk. My chest felt tight and the tears wouldn't stop falling. We sat on the floor for a while before she helped me up and led me over to the couch.

"I'm going to get you some tissues. I'll be right back."

She returned and dabbed the tissue around my eyes.

"There, there, sweet girl. Everything is going to be okay."

"No. No it's not."

"Tell me what happened."

After taking a moment to compose myself and blow my nose, I began to tell her, and I instantly felt she took his side.

"He shouldn't have done that without speaking to you first, but he did it for you, honey. I believe it was all in good intention."

"So you're taking his side and saying that I shouldn't have gotten so upset?"

"No. I'm not taking anyone's side. When two people love each other, they want to do things to make the other's person's life easier."

"No! He did it for his own selfish reasons. He wants me to see him. He can't stand the thought of being with a blind girl the rest of his life who will never see what he looks like."

"Aubrey." She pulled me into her. "I don't believe that's entirely true. He was trying to give you a gift. The gift of your eyesight back. If this doctor can help you, I don't understand why you won't talk to him."

"Because this is how my life was meant to be."

"That's not true."

"Yes, it is. Now, if you'll excuse me, I want to be alone."

"Aubrey."

"Aunt Charlotte, I mean it." I raised my voice.

She kissed my forehead and patted my hand.

"If you need anything, call me or come over."

"I will."

Chapter 33
Ethan

I was hurt. I was angry. I was sad. Rage consumed me, and as soon as I arrived home, I grabbed the bottle of scotch and a glass and took it upstairs to my bedroom. I downed two glasses in a flash, and as I looked over at the chair that sat in the corner, I noticed some of her clothes folded neatly on top of it. I couldn't believe what she said to me regarding Sophia. But most of all, I couldn't believe how upset she was with what I had done. Maybe I should have talked to her first about it, but I didn't think she was even capable of reacting the way she did. Maybe I didn't know her at all. But one fucking thing I knew for sure was that she never wanted her eyesight back, which I couldn't understand.

Over the next several days, I couldn't control my anger and my staff knew to stay away from me. In the blink of an eye, I was back to the person I hated most. I had let my guard down, let my feelings come to surface, and for what? Only to be shattered again.

I hailed a cab to Dr. Perry's office, climbed out, and went inside. There was only a brief wait as she was with another patient.

"Come on in, Ethan." She smiled. "Your phone call sounded urgent. What's going on?"

I placed my hands in my pocket and paced across the room.

"Aubrey and I broke up."

"Why?"

"I did something she didn't like and she said something I didn't like."

"Okay. Why don't you sit down and we'll talk about it?"

"I'm fine pacing around the room."

"What did you do?"

"I found and spoke to a doctor that may be able to help Aubrey get her eyesight back. I told her about it and she freaked out on me. She told me that she was happy the way she was and I only did it for my own selfish reasons."

"Did you tell her after you found the doctor or before?"

"After I met with him. She said I had no right. That is was her life."

"Did you do it for your own selfish reasons?" she asked.

"No. Of course not. I want Aubrey to see again. I want her to be able to see the things she never saw before the accident."

"Including you?"

"Of course. Who wouldn't want that, Dr. Perry? But that wasn't the main reason I got in touch with Dr. Marchetti."

"Dr. Marchetti from Boston?"

"Yes. Do you know him?"

"Yes. I've known him for years. He's one of the best eye specialists in the world."

I finally stopped pacing and took a seat across from her.

"I thought I was doing something good for her." I lowered my head and placed my hands over my face.

"You were, Ethan. There has to be some psychological reasoning as to why Aubrey doesn't want to meet with Dr. Marchetti. You said that she said something to you that you didn't like. What did she say?"

"She said that she wasn't Sophia, she didn't need saving, and that I couldn't save her, just like I couldn't save Sophia."

"I see."

"I told her that was a low blow, that we were over, and I left."

"You haven't spoken to her since?"

"No. I can't sleep. I have no appetite and I'm back to the same person I was before I met her."

"Do you miss her?"

"Of course I miss her. I love her more than anything in the world, but what she said to me showed me who she really was."

"That's not true, Ethan. People say things out of anger. She was hurt and angry that you spoke to Dr. Marchetti without talking to her first, so she threw back at you the one thing she knew would hurt you most."

"Well, that was a shit thing to do on her part. I still don't understand why she got so defensive about it."

"Like I said, there has to be some psychological thing going on. Perhaps she would feel guilty for getting her sight back from an accident that took the two people away she loved the most."

"That doesn't make sense." I sighed.

"In Aubrey's head, it does. Now I'm not saying that's what her problem is. All I'm saying is that there's some deep rooted issue she doesn't want to deal with. Give her some space and see what happens. She was in shock by what you told her. Perhaps seeing again frightens her. Let her work things out on her own."

"I have been."

"Would you be able to carry on a lifelong relationship with her if she decided she didn't want to attempt to get her eyesight back?"

"Of course I would. I love her, Dr. Perry."

"Then that is something you need to tell her."

****

Aubrey

The past few days had been the hardest days of my life. I cried every morning, taught my classes, and then came home to an empty apartment and cried myself to sleep. Ian and Penelope had seen me at my worst and I felt bad because they tried so hard to help me. I thought Ethan was different and apparently I was wrong. I was so sure and secure in the fact that he could love me the way I was.

My last class had just ended and Ian had a meeting with a student's parents, so I sat down at my desk and did some work on my computer until he was finished. As I was sitting there, I heard a light knock on the door.

"Come in," I spoke.

The door opened and I heard a woman's voice as the visitor approached me.

"Miss Callahan?" a soft voice spoke.

"Yes." I stood up from my desk.

"I just wanted to stop in and say hi. I'm Dr. Perry. We have a mutual friend in common: Ethan Klein."

"Hello, Dr. Perry." I extended my hand to her. "It's nice to meet you."

"It's nice to meet you too. I was a guest speaker for the psychology classes today and I remembered that Ethan told me you were a teacher here, so I thought I'd stop by and say hello."

"That was very nice. Thank you. Ethan spoke very highly of you."

"So how is Ethan? I haven't seen him in a while."

"I don't know. We aren't seeing each other anymore." I sat down in my chair.

"I'm sorry to hear that. I don't mean to be forward, Aubrey, but I can see that you're very upset. If you would like to talk about it, I'd be more than happy to listen."

"Thank you, Dr. Perry, but I don't want to waste your time. I'm sure you're very busy."

"Actually, I'm not. Speaking here today was the only thing I scheduled, so I'm not going to the office."

I didn't know if talking to her was the right thing to do. I'd spent so much time the past few days talking to my Aunt Charlotte, Penelope, and Ian, that I was tired of reliving what happened between me and Ethan. But she was a professional and maybe she could offer some advice on how to stop feeling the way I did.

"Ethan broke up with me after an argument we had. He did something that really hurt me and made me see that he wasn't the man I thought he was."

"What did he do?"

"He contacted a doctor who could possibly help me get my eyesight back. He did it without even telling me and then came home and sprang it on me out of nowhere. It was sneaky, undermining, and it made me very angry."

"Why did you get so angry that he did that?"

"Because he had no right." I looked down. "This is my life, not his. He can't love me like this. That's why he sought out that doctor. He wants me to get my eyesight back for him. He told me that he wants me to see him."

"Is that so wrong?" she asked.

"Not really. In a way, I get it, but he had no right doing what he did. If he can't be with me the way I am, then there's no point in us being together."

"Let me ask you something, Aubrey. Do you want to be able to see again?"

"I think about it sometimes. But losing my eyesight was my fate. It was my punishment and something I made peace with many years ago."

"I'm sorry, but I don't understand what you mean by 'it was your punishment.'"

My heart started racing at the thought of telling Dr. Perry about the accident.

"The accident was my fault and the reason my parents are dead. We were on our way to the beach and I couldn't wait to get there. It was a Saturday and my dad decided to go into the office first. He came home later than he said he would, so we got a late start. I remember being angry at him for it and as we were on our way, it started to pour down rain when it had been sunny and beautiful earlier in the afternoon. He said there was no use in going and he was going to turn around. My heart was broken because I had been promised all week that we would go to the beach. It was all I looked forward to. I started crying and yelling at him from the backseat, and I told him that it was his fault because he always put work in front of his family. My mom told me that I needed to calm down and that we'd go another day. I wouldn't accept that and I wouldn't stop crying. My father turned and looked at me and told me to stop or else. I'll never forget the look of anger on his face. He drifted into the other lane into oncoming traffic and my mother screamed at him to look out. He swerved, but it was too late. I had my hand on the seatbelt buckle and during the impact, I must have pressed it and released the seatbelt because I was thrown from the car. I woke up in the hospital to a world of darkness. The doctors told my aunt that the paramedics found me lying on the ground a few feet away from the car. I was barely alive, but they managed to save me."

"I'm so sorry, Aubrey," Dr. Perry spoke.

"So you see, Dr. Perry, the accident was my fault. If I had just accepted the fact that we couldn't go to the beach that day, things would be different. My parents would be alive and I wouldn't have lost my eyesight."

"You were a child. The accident wasn't your fault."

"But it was and losing my eyesight is something that I have to live with for the rest of my life. It's my punishment. Nothing can bring my parents back, so why should I be able to see again?" A tear fell from my eye.

"And you became angry at Ethan for wanting to take that punishment away from you?"

"Yes. I'm living my life the way I'm supposed to."

"Oh, Aubrey. I wish to God you didn't feel that way. That accident wasn't your fault, just like Sophia's death wasn't Ethan's. Didn't you tell him that it wasn't his fault?"

"Yes."

"How is that any different? Ethan believed that his actions drove Sophia into that ocean that night, just like you believe your actions caused that accident. So how can you say that Ethan wasn't responsible? There's no difference between the way you feel and the way he felt."

"It just is."

"No, sweetheart, it isn't. If you were to tell him about the accident, he would tell you it wasn't your fault, just like you told him it wasn't his fault. You've lived over half your life being visually impaired, and now, with today's advance technology, there's someone who could potentially help you see again. It's time to let the punishment go, Aubrey. If this doctor can help you, let him."

I heard my classroom door open and Ian's voice.

"Oh, I'm sorry. I didn't know you had company," he spoke.

"Ian, this is Dr. Perry. Dr. Perry, this is my friend, Ian."

"Nice to meet you, Ian. I'm going to go. Give some thought to what we talked about and if you need anything, please call me."

"Thank you. I will."

"It was nice to meet you, Aubrey. Hopefully, we'll talk again soon." She walked out of my classroom.

Chapter 34
Aubrey

I spent the next few days thinking about what Dr. Perry said. As I stood in the bathroom, in front of the mirror, I placed my hand on it and held it there for a few moments. Thoughts about what I looked like invaded my head. There was a question I needed an answer to, so I called in sick to work and headed over to Ethan's office. If he wasn't there, I'd wait for him.

Using the app his company developed, I easily found my way up to his office. Using my cane for guidance, I walked down the hallway until I stopped at a desk.

"May I help you?" a woman's voice asked.

"Is this Ethan Klein's office?"

"Yes, it is. Do you have an appointment with him?"

"No. But if he's in there, I need to speak with him."

"He's on a phone conference at the moment. May I ask your name?"

"Aubrey Callahan."

"Oh my gosh. It's so nice to finally meet you. I'm Lucy, Mr. Klein's secretary."

"It's nice to meet you, Lucy." I smiled.

"As soon as he's finished with his call, I'll let him know you're here. I'm sorry to say this, but he's been an absolute nightmare since—well, you know."

"Since we stopped seeing each other?"

"Yes. Don't get me wrong, he's always been a nightmare, but since he met you, he became a totally different person, and it was nice while it lasted. Gee, maybe I shouldn't have said that. I'm sorry."

"Don't be. I understand. He can be a difficult man."

"That's an understatement."

"LUCY!" I heard the door open and his harsh and authoritative voice spoke. "Aubrey?" His voice calmed.

"Hello, Ethan."

My nerves were getting the best of me.

"What are you doing here? Shouldn't you be at school?"

"I took the day off. I need to speak with you."

"Sure. Come on in."

"First, you need to apologize to your secretary for yelling her name the way you did," I bravely spoke as I stood there.

"Lucy, I apologize for being so abrupt."

"It's fine, Mr. Klein."

I walked into his office and he shut the door. A feeling of sickness rose in the pit of my stomach.

"Are you standing in front of me?" I asked.

"Yes. I am." His hand lightly touched my arm.

"I have a question for you and I want an honest answer."

"Okay."

"Could you be with me if I never got my eyesight back?"

"Yes, Aubrey. Of course I could, and I would. The only thing that matters to me is being with you. Fuck. Do you have any idea how hard this has been for me? How many times I've wanted to reach out to you? But I couldn't because I was afraid you'd tell me to go to hell after what I'd done."

"I do know because I've felt the same way. I'm sorry, Ethan, for the horrible things I said to you. I had no right getting so angry the way I did."

"Sweetheart, I had no right to contact Dr. Marchetti without speaking to you first." He took hold of my hand. "I've missed you so much but I wanted to give you as much space and time as you needed. I've been miserable without you."

"I have too, and I'm sorry."

"I'm sorry too, baby. I really am."

I felt his arms wrap tightly around me.

"I need you to forgive me, Aubrey."

"I do, and I need you to forgive me. There's a reason why I became so upset with you, and we can talk about that later."

"Listen, nothing in this world matters to me more than being with you. I need you in my life."

"And I need you, Ethan. I would like you to do something for me."

"I'll do anything for you."

"I want you to call Dr. Marchetti and set up an appointment to see him. I'll sign the papers so he can get my medical report from the accident because I'm ready to see if he can help me."

"Aubrey, let's just forget about him. I never should have contacted him in the first place. I want you just the way you are."

"I appreciate that, but this is my decision and I'm ready to do this. I want to do it for me."

"Are you sure?"

"Yes. I'm positive."

His grip around me tightened before he broke our embrace and our lips were locked in a passionate kiss.

"I love you so much, Aubrey Callahan."

"I love you too, Ethan." I smiled.

Before I knew it, he swooped me up and carried me out of his office.

"Lucy, clear my schedule. I'm taking the rest of the day off and I don't want to be disturbed. Call Harry and have him pull the car around."

"Have a great day, Mr. Klein," she spoke with excitement.

"What are you doing?" I giggled.

"I'm taking you back to my house and we're spending the rest of the day in bed. We have a lot of making up to do." He kissed my lips.

"I love that idea." I smiled.

****

Ethan called Dr. Marchetti and set my appointment for next Thursday. I spoke with the principal of the school and arranged to have Thursday and Friday off so I could travel to Boston. Dr. Marchetti said that we'd have the consultation on Thursday and schedule the surgery for Friday morning. The night before Ethan and I left, we had a goodbye dinner with my Aunt Charlotte, Mr. Morris, Ian and Rigby, and Penelope.

"I'm so proud of you for doing this." My aunt hugged me tight. "And even if it doesn't work, it's okay."

"I know, and I'm not getting my hopes up. But I have to try."

After saying our goodbyes, Ethan and I went back to my apartment to get my bags and take them back to his house, where we would spend the night and head to the airport first thing in the morning.

Walking into the hospital, a nervousness engulfed me. My life could change drastically in a matter of a day and I wasn't sure how to cope with it. Don't get me wrong; this was what I wanted, but nonetheless, I was still scared as shit.

"Aubrey, it's so good to finally meet you. Come here; I feel the need to give you a hug."

"It's nice to meet you, Dr. Marchetti. Thank you for agreeing to see me."

"Of course. Please have a seat."

Ethan led me over to where the chairs were and then took a seat next to me, holding my hand the entire time.

"Okay," Dr. Marchetti spoke. "First thing we need to do is an ultrasound of your eyes so I can get a better idea of what's going on. I know that the optic nerves in both eyes have been severed from the accident but I need to see if there is anything else we're dealing with. So, let's go across the hall and get this started."

Walking across the hall into another room, he had me sit down while bringing a machine up to my eyes.

"You have a lot of scar tissue that has formed, which is normal and there's a lot of inflammation. Once we remove the scar tissue and reduce the inflammation, I'm going to inject the severed nerves with mutation cells, including stem cells to try and get the nerves to regenerate. Now, I want you to know that it could take several months for you to get your vision back completely. There is a small chance, Aubrey, that this might not work. You could still either be completely blind, or you may have some residual sight."

"I understand, Dr. Marchetti. Even if it doesn't work, I'm okay with it because this is how I've lived my life. It working would only be a bonus. But trust me, I'm not getting my hopes up."

"Okay." He patted my hand. "Let's do this. Be back here tomorrow morning at five a.m. We'll get you prepped and in surgery at six. It should take around four to five hours for the procedure."

****

"Are you okay?" Ethan asked as he held me tight after we made love.

"I'm fine."

"Are you sure? You've been quiet all day."

"I'm just a little scared."

He kissed the top of my head.

"I know you are and I'd be worried if you weren't. But everything is going to be okay. Even if it doesn't work, you would have lost nothing."

"I know."

"I love you, sweetheart, and I will be right here by your side no matter what happens. I will support you, love you, and give you everything you need and want. You're stuck with me for life, whether you want to be or not."

I couldn't help but let out a light laugh. "I love you and there's no other person in the world that I would rather be stuck with." I lifted my head and kissed his lips.

"Good. Now let's get some sleep. You have a very big day tomorrow."

"Good night, Ethan." I lay my head back on his chest. "I love you."

"I love you too, baby. Good night."

Chapter 35
Ethan

The truth was that I didn't sleep a wink all night. I was worried about Aubrey's surgery. One, in case it didn't work, I didn't want her to be disappointed, and two, because Dr. Marchetti had a talk with me on the effects regaining her eyesight could have on her emotionally. He said that she would have to learn to see all over again and that could send her into a depression. He told me that it would become a developmental process, like learning a new language and to be patient with her and help her as much as I could.

I was starting to have second thoughts about the whole thing. What if this affected her teaching? I could never live with myself if she became emotionally damaged by having this surgery. The next morning, as we were getting ready to leave, I asked her if she was sure she wanted to go through with it.

"I'm sure, Ethan. Why are you asking me that?"

"Because of the effect it could have on you afterwards."

She gave me a small smile and placed her hand on the side of my face.

"I've done my research. I know all about the transition and I'll be okay. If this works, it's going to take time for my brain to catch up. I get that. Did you really think that I just thought I could see again and there would be no problems?"

"Why didn't you tell me this before?"

"Because it's nothing for you to worry about. I remember colors, numbers, shapes, objects, and words. I lived in a world of light for eight years. I understand there will some issues, but I can handle it."

"You're amazing. Did you know that?" I softly kissed her lips.

"Yeah. I am. Aren't I?" She grinned.

"You sure are." I pulled her into a tight embrace before heading to the hospital.

****

Aubrey

I could hear the sound of my name being called as I felt the bandages that were covering my eyes. I stirred and brought my hand to my face.

"It's all over, Aubrey," Dr. Marchetti spoke. "How are you feeling?"

"Tired," I whispered.

"We need to leave the bandages on for a few more hours and then we'll remove them." He grabbed hold of my hand and gave it a squeeze. "Get some rest."

"Ethan?" I softly spoke.

"I'm right here, baby." He kissed my forehead. "You did great. I'm so proud of you."

"Thanks." I attempted a half smile.

"Get some rest and let the anesthetic wear off. I'll be right here waiting for you."

I lightly nodded my head and drifted off into a sound sleep. After sleeping for what felt like several hours, I stirred, and instantly, I felt the touch of a hand on mine.

"How are you feeling?" Ethan asked.

"Better." I smiled.

"Dr. Marchetti was just in here to check up on you. He said that the bandages can come off in a couple of hours. Are you thirsty?"

"Yeah. A little bit."

"Here's some water." He held the straw to my mouth.

"Have you eaten?" I asked him.

He chuckled. "Don't worry about me. I'm fine. My mom and sister called. They wanted to see how the surgery went and to make sure you were fine."

"That was so nice of them."

"Penelope, Ian, and your Aunt Charlotte also called or should I say facetimed me to see how you were."

"You better not have let them see me in this bed."

"It was only for a second, Aubrey. I swear." He laughed. "They wanted to see for themselves how you were, plus you know Penelope; she doesn't take no for an answer."

A couple of hours had passed and I was growing more nervous by the second. My hospital room door opened and Dr. Marchetti and his team of doctors stepped inside. A sick feeling formed in the pit of my stomach. This was it and I wasn't sure if I was ready.

"Hi, Aubrey. Are you ready?"

I took in a long, deep breath as I tried to control my racing heart.

"I think so."

He raised the back of the bed so I was sitting straight up. I felt his hand start to unwrap the bandages and my palms began to sweat.

"You okay?" Ethan asked as he held my sweaty palm.

"I'm okay."

"Now I'm going to remove the metal plates from your eyes. Keep them closed until I tell you to open them. Okay, Aubrey, slowly, and I mean slowly, open your eyes."

I swallowed hard first and then carefully opened my eyes. A swoosh of light fell over me and instantly, I closed them tight.

"Aubrey, what's wrong?" Dr. Marchetti asked.

"The light. I saw light and it kind of freaked me out."

"That's understandable. Your eyes may hurt for a moment while they adjust. Try it again, but very slowly."

Ethan's grip on my hand tightened as I slowly opened my eyes and stared straight ahead. I gulped as I saw outlines of people, shadows, black and white. I slowly turned my head towards Ethan and my eyes filled with tears as, for the first time, I saw him. The outline of his face, a blurred shadow, but not too blurry that I couldn't make out his features. A tear fell from my eye as I reached up and placed my hand on his cheek and a smile graced his beautiful face.

"I love your smile."

"Everyone out. Let's give them a few moments alone," Dr. Marchetti spoke.

Ethan swallowed hard as he sat down on the edge of the bed and stared at me as he brushed a strand of hair away from my face. A tear fell from his eye and I gently wiped it away.

"You saw that?"

"Yes."

"Can you see, Aubrey? I mean, really see?"

"Not fully. I see shadows, outlines, and some colors, like the blue shirt you're wearing."

He wrapped his arms around me and pulled me into him.

"My God, this is a miracle. I love you so much."

"I love you too."

Dr. Marchetti and his team walked back in and approached me.

"How many doctors are in the room, Aubrey?" he asked.

"Including you?"

"Yes. Including me." He smiled.

"Six."

"How many fingers am I holding up?"

"Three."

He walked away from the bed and over to the door.

"Now how many?"

It was so blurry that I couldn't really make it out.

"I don't know."

While holding the same fingers up, he slowly walked towards me.

"Tell me when you can see how many fingers I'm holding up."

"Four."

"Very good."

He approached me, sat down on the other side of the bed, and placed his hand on top of mine.

"The surgery was a success. But it's going to take time. It could take months, but every day, your vision should get a little better. You're going to need some help learning to see again. I'm not too concerned about colors, shapes, numbers, and various objects because you learned all that before the accident. Your brain has to readapt to its visual surroundings. It needs to retrain itself. Don't get too frustrated if things don't come to you. You need to stay here overnight for observation and if all checks out well, you can go back to your hotel tomorrow and fly back to New York on Sunday."

Chapter 36

Ethan

I stayed with Aubrey at the hospital all night. There was no way I was leaving her. I had briefly left the room to go and get us some coffee, and when I came back, I found her in the bathroom, staring at herself in the mirror.

****

Aubrey

I wanted to wait until I was alone to see myself in the mirror. After Ethan left to go get some coffee, I climbed out of bed and made my way to the bathroom that was ten steps away. It took me a minute to be brave enough to flip the light switch for I was scared at who would be staring back at me. Placing my hand on the switch, I closed my eyes and flipped it up. Taking in a deep breath, I slowly opened my eyes. Was this me? The last time I saw myself in a mirror was when I was eight years old and had long blonde braids. Images of that little girl came to my mind and I could see the shadow of her in the mirror. I'd grown into this woman that I only knew from the inside. It was strange seeing myself after all these years. I felt like a stranger was staring back at me. A person I didn't visually recognize and it freaked me the fuck out for a moment. Until Ethan walked in.

****

Ethan

She looked frightened, like a child who was looking at a total stranger. Placing my hands on her shoulders, I smiled at her through the mirror.

"Didn't I tell you that you were gorgeous?"

"This is so strange to me, Ethan. The last time I looked in a mirror, I was a child. A little girl. And now, I'm this woman."

"Yes, sweetheart. You're this beautiful woman both inside and out."

Tears started to fall from her eyes as she turned to me and buried her face into my chest.

"It's okay, baby. Let's get you back in bed."

Just as I helped her back in bed, Wanda, her nurse, walked in shaking a small cup with a pill in it.

"I have a little something for you to take, Aubrey. Hold out your hand."

"What is this?"

"It's a little something to help you sleep. Dr. Marchetti ordered it for you. Right now, your brain is on visual overload and you won't be able to unwind." She handed her a cup of water.

Aubrey popped the pill in her mouth and chased it down with water.

"Get some sleep." Wanda smiled. "Are you staying with her?" she asked me.

"Yes."

"Good man. Do you want a cot?"

"No. I'll be sleeping in this bed with her."

"Like I said, good man." She smiled.

Aubrey moved over as I climbed in next to her and held my arm out while she snuggled against my chest and fell fast asleep while I stroked her hair.

Chapter 37
Aubrey

Slowly opening my eyes, I squinted at the sun that peered through my window, and I visually took in the room as I lay there wrapped in Ethan's arms. Staring at his face, I found that he was more handsome than I ever imagined. He was a beautiful sight. Bringing my hand up, I lightly traced his lips with my finger. Lips that kissed mine with meaning and passion. His eyes opened and he looked at me as the corners of his mouth curved upwards.

"You're staring at me."

"Get used to it." I smiled.

"Never." He kissed me.

Ethan climbed out of bed as I sat up. He went into the bathroom, washed his face, and then went to get us some coffee. I lay there, my vision just a little bit clearer. It wasn't much, but to me, it was everything. The door opened and Dr. Marchetti walked in.

"Good morning, Aubrey. How are you feeling today?"

"Morning, doctor. I'm okay."

"And your vision?"

"A little bit better than yesterday."

"Good. I need to check your eyes. The light might bother them a little bit, but I need you to hold still and try not to blink."

He shined the small white light into my right eye first and then in my left. I was nervous that he was going to tell me something wasn't right.

"Everything looks good." He grinned. "On a scale of one to ten, ten being the best, tell me how you feel."

"I'd say an eight."

"All your vitals are completely normal, so I'm going to let you go home today."

Ethan walked in the room with our coffees and set them down on the counter.

"Did I just hear you right, Dr. Marchetti?" he asked. "You're letting Aubrey go home today?"

"Yes. She's doing great and there's nothing more we can do here, so why make her uncomfortable? She'll do much better in her own surroundings and out of this hospital bed."

"Thank you, Dr. Marchetti." My grin widened.

"You're welcome, Aubrey. I would like to put your case in the journals, but I'll need your permission."

"That's fine."

"Great. I'll go get the paperwork for you to sign and you should be out of here in about thirty minutes."

After he walked out of the room, Ethan approached me and wrapped his arms around me.

"Are you ready to face the world?"

"As ready as I'll ever be." I lay my head on his shoulder with concern.

"Since we can leave today, I would like to just drive our rental car back to New York. It's only about a three-and-a-half-hour drive. What do you think?"

"I think that's a great idea. I'd much rather sit in a car than on a crowded airplane."

"Okay." He pulled out his phone. "I'll let the rental place know that we'll be driving back to New York."

I didn't want to let Ethan know that I was a little apprehensive about stepping out of the hospital and facing the world as a sighted person. There was a nervousness inside me that I didn't understand. I should be the happiest woman in the world to get my eyesight back, but something bothered me. Something I needed to keep to myself until I could work it out.

After signing the paperwork that Dr. Marchetti wanted signed, I hooked my arm around Ethan's.

"You ready?" He looked over at me.

Taking in a deep breath, I spoke, "Yes. Let's go."

As we walked to the elevator, I felt unsteady and my grip around his arm tightened.

"Is something wrong?"

"No. Nothing's wrong."

Stepping into the elevator, I looked at the panel of numbers and ran my fingers along the braille. Still holding onto Ethan's arm, I closed my eyes as the elevator took us to the lobby. Stepping out onto the carpeted floor, we headed towards the doors that would lead me into the open world. As we approached, the doors slid open and I instantly stopped. Ethan looked over at me and kissed the side of my head.

"Take your time, sweetheart. We aren't in any hurry."

I took in a long deep breath as I put one foot in front of the other and walked outside. The sun was so bright that it hurt my eyes. Splashes of green filled the surrounding area. Grass, trees, bushes, and shrubs overwhelmed me. The air was cool. I stopped and looked up at the blue sky and the white fluffy clouds that floated above it. I felt uneasy, so I pulled my cane from my bag, unfolded it, and tapped it on the ground in front of me. Ethan looked over at me but didn't say word. He couldn't possibly understand what I was feeling.

He led me over to a black car and opened the door for me. I climbed in and when the door shut, I felt lost. Closing my eyes, I pulled the seatbelt over me and buckled it. *It's going to take time*, I silently chanted to myself over and over again. Ethan climbed in on the driver's side and took hold of my hand, bringing it up to his lips.

We arrived at the hotel, and when we walked through the doors and entered the lobby, people were everywhere; talking, laughing, babies crying, in the door, out the door. Phones were ringing, carts with luggage were being pushed in every direction. My brain was on visual stimulation overload, so I shut my eyes and reverted into my world of darkness. Once we stepped out of the elevators and onto our floor, there was quiet, so I opened my eyes as Ethan led me down the hallway to our room. Pushing the card key into the lock, he opened the door and I stepped inside.

"What do you think of the room?" he asked.

"The same thing I thought about it when we first arrived. It's big."

He chuckled. "What about the décor? Do you like it?"

"Yes. I do like it," I replied as I stared at the wall and the carpet that had flowers on it. "Is it okay if I take a quick shower before we head back?"

"Of course. I'm going to call your aunt and friends and let them know we'll be coming home today."

"Okay." I gently smiled as I walked to the bathroom.

I started the shower and stripped out of my clothes: a pair of capri jeans and a red tank top. Before stepping into the shower, I turned and faced the mirror as I looked at my naked body. Bringing my hands up to my breasts, I stared at them and then ran them down my abdomen. Ethan stood and looked at me from the doorway.

"You're so beautiful." He smiled as he walked up behind me and placed his hands on my hips, while giving my shoulder a soft kiss. "Would you mind if I took a shower with you?"

I could feel the hardness of his cock press against my lower back and a deep ache between my legs formed.

"Not at all." I gave a half smile.

I stepped into the shower and let the water stream down on me while Ethan stripped out of his clothes. I was a little scared to see his manhood since I'd never seen one before. I knew it by touch, and believe me, I touched it all the time, but to actually be able to see it frightened me a bit.

He opened the glass door and stepped in front of me. Instantly, my eyes looked down at his cock, which was standing tall, straight, and thick. It looked as powerful as it felt when he was inside me. His left hand groped my breast as his right hand placed itself between my legs. Looking into my eyes, he slipped his finger inside me and dipped his head, brushing his lips against mine. My hand wrapped around his cock and began moving up and down his shaft. A low moan rumbled in his chest as he threw his head back and closed his eyes. I lightly pushed his body back against the tiled wall and he removed his fingers from me.

"What are you doing?" he asked with bated breath.

"I want to see you come."

He grabbed the sides of my face and smashed his mouth into mine, kissing me more passionately than he ever had before. Slowing down my speed, I loosened my grip around him and lightly moved my hand up and down the tip of him. Cries of pleasure escaped from inside him as his cock erupted all over my hand. I looked up at him, and our eyes locked. He grabbed my wrists and, in a split second, he had me pinned up against the tile, arms above my head. His mouth devoured my breasts and his teeth clamped around my hard nipples. He slid his tongue down my torso, let go of my wrists, got down on his knees, and explored my most sensitive spot. My hands gripped his head as the water beat down on him. Before, I could only feel, and now, I could see what he did to me, what I did to him. He stood up, his fingers gripping my ass, and lifted me up, forcing my legs around him. His cock thrust inside me and I gasped.

"Keep looking at me while I'm fucking you," he spoke heatedly.

I stared into his beautiful green eyes. My heart melted at that moment as I watched the expression on his face as he moved in and out of me. I tightened my legs around him and bit down on my bottom lip as the force of my orgasm exploded around him. He moaned as he kept thrusting while staring into my eyes.

"I love you," he whispered breathlessly.

"I love you too."

His movement slowed and he suddenly halted as I watched the look on his face while he came inside me. He lowered his head and tried to catch his breath. Setting me down, he pulled me into an embrace and held me as if he was never letting go.

Once our shower was finished, we stepped out and he wrapped a towel around me before getting one for himself. He kissed my lips one last time, wrapped a towel around his waist and walked into the bedroom. I walked over to the sink and stared at my wet self in the mirror. Looking down at a black bag that held my makeup, I began to go through it, checking out the two-color eyeshadow palette and the pink blush that sat inside. I picked up my foundation bottle, removed the cap, and stared at it. Closing my eyes, I began to apply it, like I always did. It felt more comfortable that way. I swept a brown shadow across my eye, a touch of blush across my cheeks, and applied a light coat of mascara.

Chapter 38
Ethan

I stood in the doorway of the bathroom and watched as Aubrey applied her makeup with her eyes closed. I had grown concerned because I noticed she did that a lot today. Stepping out onto the balcony, I gave Dr. Marchetti a call.

"Dr. Marchetti."

"Hi, doctor, it's Ethan Klein."

"Hello, Ethan. Is everything okay?"

"Yeah. I just have some concerns."

"Okay. What's going on?"

"Aubrey's been closing her eyes a lot and when we left the hospital, she pulled out her cane and used it."

"Were her eyes closed while she was using her cane?"

"No."

"You need to remember that Aubrey has used nothing but touch sensory for the past seventeen years. To her, that's her life, her routine, and what makes her feel safe. It's going to take time for her to physically and emotionally adjust. Each day, she should start becoming less dependent on touch. It's nothing to worry about, Ethan. Just do your best to make her feel safe during the transition."

"Thank you, Dr. Marchetti. I will."

Ending the call, I placed my phone in my pocket and walked back into the suite.

"Who were you talking to?" Aubrey asked.

"Rob. There was an issue with something at the office."

"Is everything okay?"

"Everything's fine now." I walked over and gave her a kiss. "You should get dressed. We need to get going."

She walked over to her suitcase and pulled out the two sets of clothes she had packed. She set them on the bed and looked them over.

"What's wrong?"

"Nothing. It's just weird to actually see my clothes. I can't wait to see my closet and to see if anyone has steered me wrong over the years." She smirked.

I couldn't help but smile as she removed her towel and pulled on her jeans and a navy blue shirt over her head.

****

Aubrey

The drive home was a little difficult. I took in as much of the scenery as I could handle, but shut my eyes for a while to give my mind a rest. Ethan tried to comfort me the best he could by holding my hand and making me laugh with his jokes. Some of which weren't that funny, but I humored him anyway.

He pulled up to the curb of a building and I looked over at him.

"This is where you live." He smiled as he gave my hand a squeeze.

Climbing out of the car, I studied the tall tan building with the glass revolving door. I saw an older gentleman, about six feet tall with white hair, come out from the building with a smile on his face.

"Welcome back, Aubrey."

The minute I heard his voice I knew it was Kale, the doorman. He walked over and took our bags from Ethan.

"Good day, Mr. Klein." He smiled.

"Kale." I grinned as he turned to me. "It's so good to see you after all these years."

He chuckled. "Well, it's only been a couple of days."

"Aubrey and I flew to Boston and she had surgery on her eyes. She has most of her vision back," Ethan spoke.

"Oh my God, Aubrey. Is that true? Can you really see me?"

"Yes, and you're a very handsome man." I placed my hand on his cheek.

"Come here, girl," he spoke with excitement as he set our bags down and hugged me. "You didn't mention you were having surgery."

"I didn't want to tell anyone in case it didn't work."

"This is a miracle. I'm so happy for you."

"Thank you." I smiled.

As we stepped out of the elevator and headed to my apartment, I was a nervous wreck, for I wasn't emotionally prepared to see my Aunt Charlotte yet. Ethan slid the key in the lock and when he opened the door and I stepped inside a place that had been my home and safe haven for the past several years, it felt different. It almost felt as though I stepped into unfamiliar territory. But I was going to embrace it. This was my home and to be able to see the couch I sat on, the table I ate at, the kitchen I cooked in, and the bed that I slept in was all surreal.

"Wow. Look at this place." I smiled as I wiped a tear from my eye.

"It's pretty cool. Isn't it?" Ethan hooked his arm around me and kissed the side of my head.

"Yeah. It's pretty cool."

Suddenly, there was knock at the door.

"It's your family and friends," Ethan spoke. "I told them to give you a few minutes before coming over. I hope you don't mind. They really want to see you."

"I really want to see them too."

I took in a deep breath and swallowed hard as Ethan opened the door. My Aunt Charlotte walked in first. How did I know that was my Aunt Charlotte? She was an older woman with the same blonde hair I remembered her having when I was eight years old.

"Hi, Aunt Charlotte." I smiled as I stared directly at her.

She cupped her mouth with her hand as her eyes swelled with tears. Walking over to me, she placed her hands on each side of my face and slowly nodded her head as she fought to hold back the tears.

"Finally," she whispered as she pulled me into a tight embrace.

"It's so good to see you, Aunt Charlotte."

"My baby girl. I can't believe this." She broke our embrace and once again placed her hands on each side of my face.

I looked behind her and my eyes locked with Penelope's. She walked her teary eyed self over my way.

"You are gorgeous." I smiled as I hugged her.

And that she was with her long red wavy hair, emerald eyes, and perfect snow white skin.

"I can't believe this, Aubrey," she cried. "Oh my God. I just can't believe it."

"My turn," Ian spoke as he grabbed me and hugged me.

Ian looked exactly as my mind had pictured him. Tall, tanned, spikey brown hair, chocolate eyes, and black-rimmed glasses that suited his face.

"You're sexy. Rigby is a lucky guy." I smiled.

He wiped the uncontrollable tears that streamed down his face.

"Now I'm not going to be able to make faces at you."

I laughed. "You still can and I'll make them right back."

The best part of getting my eyesight back wasn't seeing the sight of the beauty of the world. It was seeing the people I loved more than life.

Chapter 39
Aubrey

Two Months Later

Life was a huge adjustment after the operation, and to this day, I still found myself closing my eyes every once in a while, just so I could go back to the world that made me who I had become. With each sun that rose, my eyesight and the clarity of the world became better. One of the best times I had was going shopping with Penelope for new clothes and shoes. I would admit that my taste in style had changed now that I had sight. Ethan took me to Shakespeare Garden a couple of days after I returned home and it was exactly how I visualized it in my mind. It still gave me a sense of peace, and before the weather had turned too cold, Ethan and I would go every Saturday morning with our coffees in hand, where we sit on a blanket in the grass and I would read while he laid his head on my lap and listened. When I returned back to school a week after my operation, my students overwhelmed me with their kindness by throwing me a welcome back party. To see their bright smiling faces was pure joy.

It was now December and I awoke earlier than usual for a Saturday morning. I needed to use the bathroom, so I carefully rolled out from under Ethan's arm and quietly made my way across the room. When I was finished, I walked over to the bedroom window and peeked through the curtains. My eyes widened and I let out a loud sound.

"What's wrong?" Ethan quickly sat up.

"Oh my God!" I cupped my mouth with my hand.

"What? Aubrey, are you okay?" he asked in a panicked voice.

"It's snowing!" I exclaimed as I looked over at him.

He fell back down and pulled the sheet over him. Going into his closet where I kept some of my clothes, I quickly pulled on a pair of leggings and an oversized cream-colored cable knit sweater.

"What are you doing?" he asked as he opened one eye.

"I'm going outside." I pulled on my socks.

"Sweetheart, we'll go later. I promise. Come back to bed."

"Fuck later, Ethan. It's snowing, and for the first time, I can see it. I'm going now!"

Walking over to the bed, I kissed his forehead. "Go back to sleep."

I raced down the stairs to the front door and put on my tall boots and my winter coat. Stepping outside on the porch, I looked out into the city, which was covered in a white blanket. Soft large flakes hit my face as I made my way down the steps. It brought back a memory I had when I was six years old. I sat on the steps and watched as the flakes hit the ground and stuck to it. A few moments later, Ethan took a seat next to me.

"I told you to go back to sleep." I smiled.

"How could I knowing how excited you were about the snow." He kissed my cheek and took my hand.

"I remember when I was a kid, my father traveled to Colorado for a business trip and was stuck there for a couple days due to a snow storm that hit. When he returned, I asked him to tell me all about the snow. He reached into his bag and pulled out a snow globe, turned it upside down, and told me that's what it looked like. I'll never forget how I just sat and stared it. When it was done, I shook it again, over and over. He told me that one day, he'd take me up to the mountains to see it. We never did get around to making that trip."

"Well, now you see it. Is it as beautiful as you thought it would be?"

"It is." I grinned.

Ethan brought my hand up to his lips. "I have an idea. Let's walk down to Starbucks and get some coffee."

"Seriously?" My face lit up.

"Yeah. Just let me go change first. I'll be right back." He jumped up and went inside.

When he returned, I laced my fingers in his and we walked in the snow to get some coffee. This day was as perfect as could be.

****

Later that night, Ethan told me that we were going out, but he wouldn't tell me where. He said it was a surprise and not to ruin it by asking so many questions. We originally had plans with Charles and Lexi, but Ethan cancelled them, which I thought was kind of rude, but he didn't seem to care. As I was putting the final touches on my makeup, and Ethan was standing next to me shaving, looking as sexy as he always did, I glared at him.

"What?" He looked at me through the mirror with a narrowing eye.

"I still can't believe you cancelled our dinner plans with Charles and Lexi."

"Are you still bothered by that?"

"Yes."

"Well, don't be. Charles said it was perfectly fine and we'll get together next weekend."

"I still think it was rude."

"I know you do because you keep telling me that." He smirked.

"So whatever you have planned better be worth canceling on our friends at the last minute."

"I guess we'll have to wait and see. Won't we?" He winked.

His smug attitude was getting on my nerves.

"Since you won't tell me where we're going, I don't know what to wear."

"I've already laid out your clothes on the bed. Dammit!" He nicked his face.

"Are you okay?"

He sighed. "Yeah." He reached for a tissue.

"I would say that was karma getting you back for canceling on our friends." I smiled as I patted his ass and walked out of the bathroom.

Walking into the bedroom, I saw there was a pair of jeans and a pink sweater lying on the bed. I couldn't help but smile at the fact that he actually picked out my clothes for me.

"Are you ready?" he asked as he stood by the door with his hand on the knob.

"Yes." I smiled. "Let's go."

Harry pulled up to the curb in front of a donut shop and Ethan climbed out and opened the door for me.

"So, you cancelled dinner with our friends so we could get some donuts?" I smirked.

"Very funny, Aubrey." He held out his arm for me.

Hooking mine around his, we walked down the snow-covered street and over a block until we reached one of the entrances to Central Park. I was so busy looking at how pretty the city was covered in snow that I didn't even notice the horse and carriage that was in front of me.

"Your carriage awaits you, my princess." Ethan smiled.

"Wait. We're going on a horse and carriage ride?"

"We are." He nodded. "Through Central Park."

"Why?" I asked as I climbed into the carriage.

"Because it's been snowing all day and the park is really beautiful covered in snow. I thought since you are so weirdly excited about seeing it, what better way than sitting in a carriage?" He smiled.

"So this is why you cancelled our plans with Charles and Lexi." I placed my hand on his cheek.

"Do you forgive me?"

"I so forgive you, Mr. Klein." My lips brushed against his.

Central Park was a blanket of white and truly a sight that I would never take for granted, from the covered pathways to the snow-topped trees and the lightly snow-covered street lamps that glistened from afar. I held on to Ethan tight as he wrapped his arm around me, taking in the beautiful scenery that could easily be a picture on a Christmas card. I was so happy and so in love with him and tonight was the perfect date night. He took something he knew excited me and turned it into something I would never forget.

When we approached Shakespeare Garden, the carriage stopped and Ethan climbed out. Holding his hand out to me, I placed mine in his, and we began to take a stroll.

"I thought maybe you'd like to see Shakespeare Garden covered in snow." He smiled.

"It's so pretty, Ethan. Thank you for doing this for me." I laid my head on his shoulder.

"You're welcome. I'd do anything for you." His lips pressed against my head.

We approached the area that we used to sit at every Saturday morning before it got too cold to come anymore, and Ethan took his glove-covered hand and wiped away the snow from a bench.

"Have a seat," he spoke.

As soon as I sat down, he took hold of both my hands and got down on his knees.

"Aubrey, I just wanted to tell you that I love you so much and I couldn't imagine my life without you. You have taken me to a whole new level of living. My world was so dark before I met you and with one smile, you drove that darkness away. You are the most beautiful woman in the world, both inside and out. I'm a changed man because of you and I'm who I'm supposed to be. I'm the man who is going to love you for the rest of your life. Will you marry me, Aubrey?" He reached into his pocket and pulled out a small blue velvet box, opened the lid, and held up the most beautiful diamond ring I'd ever imagined.

My hand flew to my mouth in shock as my heart pounded out of my chest.

"Yes! Yes, Ethan. I will marry you." My eyes filled with tears.

With a smile on his face, he placed the ring on my finger and brought it up to his lips, and then picked me up from the bench, kissed my mouth, and swung me around.

"Do you know how happy you've made me?" he asked with excitement.

"I hope as happy as you've made me."

"I love you so much, Aubrey, and I promise to love you forever."

"And I promise to love you forever, Ethan."

Our lips locked tightly together as we stood under the light snow that trickled down from the sky and gently landed on us as our first passionate kiss as an engaged couple would never be forgotten.

****

Ethan

Aubrey and I were married seven months later in Central Park. She was a stunning bride and I had never seen a more beautiful woman in my entire life. She lit up my world so bright and gave me the most precious gift of all: her love.

Shortly after we were married, we opened up a school in Manhattan called Klein School for the Blind. It was divided into two sections. One section was for children and their education, and the other was for people who had lost their sight at a later age and needed help learning how to live their daily lives as a visually impaired person. With the help of my astounding tech team, we continued to develop new technology to make the lives of those who couldn't see easier and the world a better place to live.

Aubrey, my company, and the school were everything I needed in life. Or so I thought, until the day she told me that I was going to be a father and, later, when I held my daughter in my arms for the first time. She was the spitting image of her mother, right down to her cute little button nose. They were my existence and I thanked God every day for putting me in Aubrey's path. If it wasn't for her, I would still be a lost soul in a dark world, living a life with no meaning.

About The Author

Sandi Lynn is a New York Times, USA Today and Wall Street Journal bestselling author who spends all of her days writing. She published her first novel, Forever Black, in February 2013 and hasn't stopped writing since. Her addictions are shopping, going to the gym, romance novels, coffee, chocolate, margaritas, and giving readers an escape to another world.

Please come connect with her at:

www.facebook.com/Sandi.Lynn.Author

www.twitter.com/SandilynnWriter

www.authorsandilynn.com

www.pinterest.com/sandilynnWriter

www.instagram.com/sandilynnauthor

https://www.goodreads.com/author/show/6089757.Sandi_Lynn

Made in the USA
Columbia, SC
18 February 2021

33125947R00153